Herbert Allen Hall, Jr.
Nov. 2

D1497449

Deborah Anne Hall
Aug. 16 = 44 —

Pinocchio
The Adventures
of a Marionette

By
C. Collodi
Translated from
The Italian by
Walter S. Cramp
With Editorial
Revision by
Sara E. H. Lockwood
With Many Original
Drawings by
Charles Copeland

Ginn And Company
Boston ~ New York
Chicago ~ London ~

PREFACE

Under the assumed name of C. Collodi, Carlo Lorenzini is well known to the reading world of Italy. His most successful book, *Pinocchio*, was written for children, and has already become a classic. Of all the fairy stories of Italian literature this is the best known and the best loved. The name of the marionette hero is familiar in every household of northern and central Italy. In its whimsical extravagance, its quaint humor, and its narrative style the story appeals strongly to both old and young.

American children, who have long delighted in French and German fairy tales, and among whom Hans Christian Andersen is universally beloved, should not remain in ignorance of this Italian classic. The Florentines call it a literary jewel, and as such it should be known to all young readers. In order to preserve the unique flavor of the story as much as possible the translator has followed the original rather closely. Pinocchio's waywardness and love of mischief are fully set forth, and the moral, though sufficiently obvious, is not allowed to detract from the enjoyment of his adventures.

The story is one that readily lends itself to the fertile fancy and skillful pencil of an able illustrator. In the present volume, as in the original, the pictures play an important part which is not likely to be overlooked by the readers for whom the book is designed.

PINOCCHIO

CHAPTER I

Once upon a time there was —

"A king?" my little readers will immediately say.

No, children, you are mistaken. Once upon a time there was a piece of wood. It was not fine wood, but a simple piece of wood from the wood yard, — the kind we put in the stoves and fireplaces so as to make a fire and heat the rooms.

I do not know how it happened, but one beautiful day a certain old woodcutter found a piece of this kind of wood in his shop. The name of the old man was Antonio, but everybody called him Master Cherry on account of the point of his nose, which was always shiny and purplish, just like a ripe cherry.

3

As soon as Master Cherry saw that piece of wood he was overjoyed; and rubbing his hands contentedly, he mumbled to himself, "This has come in very good time. I will make it into a table leg."

No sooner said than done. He quickly took a sharpened ax to raise the bark and shape the wood; but when he was on the point of striking it he stopped with his arm in the air, because he heard a tiny, thin little voice say, "Do not strike so hard!"

Just imagine how surprised good old Master Cherry was! He turned his bewildered eyes around the room in order to see whence that little voice came; but he saw no one. He looked under the bench, and no one was there; he looked in a sideboard which was always closed; he looked in the basket of chips and shavings; he opened the door in order to glance around his house; still he could see no one. What then?

"I understand," he said, laughing and scratching his wig; "I imagined I heard that little voice. I will begin to work again."

He took up the ax and gave the piece of wood another hard blow.

"Oh! you have hurt me!" cried the little voice, as if in pain.

This time Master Cherry was dumb. His eyes were nearly popping out of his head; his mouth was opened wide, and his tongue hung down on his chin, like that of a gorgon head on a fountain.

As soon as he could speak he said, trembling and stammering from fright, "But where does that little voice come from that says 'Oh'? There is nothing alive in this room. Can it be that this piece of wood has learned to cry and scream like

a baby ? I cannot believe it. This is an ordinary piece of wood for the fireplace, like all other pieces with which we boil a pot of beans. What next ? What if there is some one hidden inside ? If there is, so much the worse for him. I will settle him." And saying this, he seized with both hands the poor piece of wood and knocked it against the wall.

Then he stopped to listen, so as to hear if any voice complained. He waited two minutes, and heard nothing; five minutes, and nothing; ten minutes, and nothing.

"I understand," he said, forcing a laugh and rubbing his wig ; "I imagined that I heard a voice cry 'Oh!' I will begin to work again." And because he was somewhat frightened, he tried to hum an air so as to make himself courageous.

At the same time he stopped working with the ax and took up a plane to make the wood even and clean ; but while he planed he heard again the little voice, this time in a laughing tone, "Stop ! you are taking the skin off my body."

This time poor Master Cherry fell down as if shot. When he opened his eyes he found himself sitting on the ground. His face expressed utter amazement, and the end of his nose, which was always purple, became blue from great fear.

CHAPTER II

At this moment there was a knock at the door.

"Come in," said the woodcutter, without having strength enough to arise.

Then a lively old man called Geppetto entered the room.

"Good morning, Master Antonio," said Geppetto. "What are you doing on the ground?"

"I am teaching the ants their A B C's. What has brought you here, brother Geppetto?"

"I have come to ask a favor of you, Master Antonio."

"Here I am, prompt to serve you!" replied the woodcutter, raising himself on his knees.

"This morning I had an idea."

"Let me hear it."

"I thought that I would make a pretty wooden marionette; I mean a wonderful marionette, one

that can dance, walk, and jump. With this marionette I wish to travel through the world and earn
for myself a little bread."

"What then, brother Geppetto, can I do for
you?"

"I should like a piece of wood to make a marionette. Will you give it to me?"

Master Antonio gladly took up the piece of wood
that had frightened him so. But when he was
about to hand it to Geppetto the piece of wood
gave a spring, and, slipping violently from his
hands, fell and struck the shins of poor Geppetto.

"Ah! you are very polite when you give pres-
ents! Truly, Master Antonio, you have nearly
lamed me."

"I swear to you that I did not do it."

"Surely it was you who threw the piece of wood
at my legs."

"I did not throw it. The fault is all in this
wood."

"Truly?"

"Truly!"

Upon that Geppetto took the piece of wood in
his arms and, thanking Master Antonio, went home,
limping all the way.

CHAPTER III

Geppetto's home consisted of one room on the ground floor. It received light from a window under a staircase. The furniture could not have been more simple, — a broken chair, a hard bed, and a dilapidated table. On one side of the room there was a fireplace with wood burning; but the fire was painted, and above it there was also painted a boiling pot with clouds of steam all around it that made it quite real.

As soon as he entered Geppetto began to make a marionette. "What name shall I give

9

him?" he said to himself. "I think I will call him Pinocchio. That name will bring with it good fortune. I have known a whole family called Pinocchio. Pinocchio was the father, Pinocchio was the mother, and the children were called little Pinocchios, and everybody lived well. It was a happy family."

When he had found the name for the marionette he began to work with a will. He quickly made the forehead, then the hair, and then the eyes. After he had made the eyes, just imagine how surprised he was to see them look around, and finally gaze at him fixedly! Geppetto, seeing himself looked at by two eyes of wood, said to the head, "Why do you look at me so, eyes of wood?"

No response.

After he had made the eyes he made the nose; but the nose began to grow, and it grew, grew, grew, until it became a great big nose, and Geppetto thought it would never stop. He tried hard to stop it, but the more he cut at it the longer that impertinent nose became.

After the nose he made the mouth. The mouth was hardly finished when it commenced to sing and laugh. "Stop laughing," said Geppetto, vexed; but it was like talking to the wall. "Stop laughing,

I tell you," he said again in a loud tone. Then the features began to make grimaces.

Geppetto feigned not to see this impertinence and continued to work. After the mouth he made the chin, then the neck, then the shoulders, then the body, then the arms and hands.

Hardly had he finished the hands when Geppetto felt his wig pulled off. He turned quickly, and what

do you think he saw? — his yellow wig in the hands of the marionette! "Pinocchio! give me back my wig immediately," said the old man. But Pinocchio, instead of giving back the wig, put it on his own head, making himself look half smothered.

At this disobedience Geppetto looked very sad, a thing he had never done before in all his life.

Turning to Pinocchio, he said : " Bad little boy ! You are not yet finished and already lack respect to your father. Bad, bad boy ! " And he dried a tear.

There were now only the legs and feet to make. Scarcely were they finished when they began to kick poor Geppetto. " It is my fault," he said to himself ; " I ought to have thought of this at first ! Now it is too late ! " Then he took the mario-nette in his arms and placed him on the ground to make him walk. Pinocchio behaved at first as if his legs were asleep and he could not move them. Geppetto led him around the room for some time, showing him how to put one foot in front of the other. When his legs were stretched Pinocchio began to walk and then to run around the room. When he saw the door open he jumped into the street and ran away.

Poor Geppetto ran as fast as he could, but he was not able to catch him ; Pinocchio jumped like a rabbit. He made a noise with his wooden feet on the hard road like twenty pair of little wooden shoes.

" Stop him ! stop him ! " cried Geppetto ; but the people in the street, seeing the wooden mario-nette running as fast as a rabbit, stopped to look at it, and laughed, and laughed, and laughed, so that it is really hard to describe how they enjoyed it all.

Finally, through good fortune, a soldier appeared, who, hearing all the noise, thought that some colt had escaped from its master. He planted himself in the middle of the road and with a fixed look determined to catch the runaway. Pinocchio, when he saw the soldier in the road, tried to pass between his legs, but he could not do it. The soldier, scarcely moving his body, seized the marionette by the nose (which was a very ridiculous one, just the size to be seized by a soldier) and consigned him to the hands of Geppetto, who tried to correct him by pulling his ears. But just imagine — when he searched for the ears he could not find them! Do you know why? Because, in the haste of making Pinocchio, he did not finish carving them.

Taking him by the neck, Geppetto led him back, saying as he did so, "When we get home I must punish you."

Pinocchio, at this threat, threw himself on the ground and refused to walk farther. Meanwhile the curious people and the loungers began to stop and surround them. First one said something, then another. "Poor marionette!" said one of them, "he is right not to want to go back to his home. Who knows how hard Geppetto beats him?" And others added maliciously: "That Geppetto appears to be a kind man, but he is a tyrant with boys. If he gets that poor marionette in his hands, he will break him in pieces."

Altogether they made so much noise that the soldier gave Pinocchio back his liberty and took to prison instead the poor old man, who, not finding words at first with which to defend himself, wept bitterly, and on approaching the prison stammered out: "Wicked son! and to think I tried so hard to make a good marionette! I ought to have thought of all this at first."

What happened afterward is a story so strange that you will hardly believe it. However, I will tell it to you in the following chapters.

CHAPTER IV

I will tell you then, children, that while poor old Geppetto was led to prison without having done any wrong, that rogue Pinocchio, being free, took to his heels and ran toward the fields in order more easily to reach his house. In his haste he jumped high mounds of earth, hedges of thorns, and ditches of water, just as rabbits and deer do when chased by hunters.

When he arrived before the house he found the door to the street half shut. He pushed it open, entered the room, and bolted the door. Then he threw himself down on the floor and heaved a great big sigh of happiness.

But his happiness did not last very long for soon he heard some one crying in the room—"Cri-cri-cri!"

"Who is speaking to me?" said Pinocchio, frightened.

"It is I."

Pinocchio turned around and saw a large cricket that walked slowly up on the wall.

"Tell me, Cricket, who are you?"

"I am the Talking Cricket, and I have lived in this room for more than a hundred years."

"To-day, however, this room is mine," said the marionette, "and if you wish to do me a favor, go away immediately, without even turning yourself around once."

"I will not go away from here," said the Cricket, "without telling you a great truth."

"Tell it to me and be gone."

"Woe to boys who rebel against their parents, and who foolishly run away from their homes. They will never get along well in the world, and sooner or later will bitterly repent of their actions."

"Sing on, little Cricket, if it pleases you; but I know that to-morrow, at the dawn of day, I shall go away, because if I remain here, what happens to all other boys will happen to me. I shall have to go to school and be made to study; and I will tell you in confidence that I have no wish to study at all, and I propose to play and run after butterflies and climb trees and take the little birds out of their nests."

"Poor little stupid thing! Do you not know that in doing so you will become a donkey, and that everybody will make fun of you?"

"Be quiet, you dismal little Cricket!" cried Pinocchio.

But the Cricket, who was a patient philosopher, instead of becoming angry at this impertinence, continued in the same tone of voice: "And if it does not please you to go to school, why not at least learn a trade, so as to be able to earn honestly a piece of bread?"

"Do you wish me to tell you?" replied Pinocchio, who began to lose patience; "because among the trades of the world there is only one that suits my genius."

"And what trade may that be?"

"That of eating, drinking, sleeping, and amusing myself, and of living, from morning to night, an easy life."

"Those who live that way," said the Talking Cricket with his usual calmness, "always end in the hospital or in prison."

"Take care, Cricket, take care! If you make me angry I pity you."

"Poor Pinocchio! you make me pity you."

"Why do I make you pity me?"

"Because you are a marionette; and, what is worse, you have a wooden head."

At these words Pinocchio jumped up enraged, and taking a hammer from a bench flung it at the Talking Cricket.

Perhaps he did not intend to do such a thing; but unfortunately the hammer struck the poor little Cricket in the head and killed him.

CHAPTER V

Meanwhile the night came on, and Pinocchio, remembering that he had eaten nothing, felt a gnawing in his stomach that strongly resembled an appetite. Now the appetite of boys increases very quickly, and so after a few minutes the appetite became hunger, and the hunger finally became like that of a wolf.

Poor Pinocchio ran suddenly to the fireplace, where there was a pot of boiling water into which he tried to look; but he found that it was only a painting. Imagine his surprise! His nose, which was already long, began to grow longer, nearly equal to four fingers. Then he ran around the room and rummaged through all the drawers and boxes and all the hiding places in search of a piece of bread,—only a little piece of dried bread, a crust, a bone for a dog, a little mush, a fish bone, a kernel of a cherry, in fact anything at all to eat; but he found absolutely nothing.

Meanwhile his hunger constantly increased. Poor Pinocchio had no other relief than that of yawning, and he gaped with so much energy that the corners of his mouth touched his ears. Then he began to feel faint and dizzy. Weeping and despairing, he said: "The Talking Cricket was right. I have behaved badly in turning my back on my papa and running away. If my papa were only here now, I should not find myself dying of hunger. Oh! what a horrible feeling it is!"

Suddenly it appeared to him that he saw something on the top of a rubbish heap that very much resembled a hen's egg. It required but a second to jump to the spot and there he really saw a nice big egg.

It is impossible to describe the joy of the marionette. It is necessary to be a marionette in order to understand it. Fearing that it might be a dream, he turned the egg around in his hands and touched it and kissed it, and kissing it said: "And now, how ought I to cook it? Shall I make an omelet? No, it is better to poach it; or would it not be more savory to scramble it? Or instead of cooking it, I might drink it raw. No, the nicest way is to cook it in a saucepan."

No sooner said than done. He placed a saucepan above a heap of burning shavings. In the saucepan, instead of oil or butter, he put a little water. When the water began to smoke — *tac !* —

he broke the shell of the egg and held it over the steaming saucepan. He was in the act of pouring out the egg, when instead of the yolk there appeared a little chicken, very lively and polite. It made a beautiful bow and said: "Many thanks, Mr. Pinocchio, for saving me the trouble of breaking my shell. Good-by! Be good and give my respects to the family."

Saying this, the little chick spread its wings and flew out of the open window and away so quickly that it was soon out of sight.

The poor marionette remained there stupefied, with his eyes fixed, with his mouth open, and with the eggshell in his hands. He soon came to himself, however, and began to weep, to scream, and to stamp his feet on the ground in desperation, and while weeping he said: "Oh, yes! the Talking Cricket was right. If I had not run away, and if my papa were only here, I should not find myself dying of hunger. Ah! what a horrible sickness hunger is!"

And because he was more uncomfortable than ever, and because he did not know what else to do, he thought that he would go out and run to the little neighboring town, in the hope of finding some charitable person who would help him and give him a piece of bread.

CHAPTER VI

It was a horrible night. It thundered very heavily and it lightened as if the heavens would take fire, while an ugly wind whistled savagely and raised an immense cloud of dust.

Pinocchio was afraid of thunder and lightning, but his hunger was greater than his fear. In a few hundred jumps he arrived at the edge of the town, quite out of breath. He was faint and weak with hunger and fright. But he found the town all dark and deserted. The stores were closed; the doors of the houses were shut and the windows were bolted; there was not even a dog in the streets; it seemed as if the town were dead.

Then Pinocchio despairingly pulled a doorbell of one of the houses and rang it with all his might, saying to himself, "Some one will come."

Soon a cross old man with a nightcap on his head looked out of a window and cried, "What do you want at this hour?"

"Will you please give me a little bread?"

"Go away," replied the old man, believing that he had to deal with some of the bad boys who go around at night disturbing people by ringing their bells.

Poor Pinocchio returned home, weak from hunger and tired out; and because he had not enough strength to stand upright, he dropped into a chair. Resting his feet on the stove that was filled with burning shavings, he fell asleep. But while he slept, his feet, which were of wood, took fire and slowly became cinders. Pinocchio, however, snored away just as if his feet belonged to some one else.

He was awakened the next morning by some one knocking at the door.

"Who is there?" he asked, yawning and rubbing his eyes.

"It is I," replied a voice.

The voice was the voice of Geppetto.

CHAPTER VII

Poor Pinocchio, who was not quite awake, did not notice that his feet had been burned off. He gave a start and jumped down from his chair so as to run and open the door. Instead, after staggering two or three times, he fell flat on the floor; and in falling he made the same noise that a sack of wood would make in falling from the fifth story of a house.

"Open the door," cried Geppetto, from the street.

"I cannot, Father," responded the marionette, weeping and turning over and over on the floor.

"Why?"

"Because some one has eaten my feet."

"And who has eaten them?"

"The cat," said Pinocchio, seeing the cat playing with a bit of wood.

"Open the door, I say," repeated Geppetto; "if not, when I come into the house I shall whip you."

"I cannot stand up, believe me. Oh! poor, poor me! I shall be obliged to walk on my knees all my life."

Geppetto, believing that all the weeping was simply a trick to deceive him, thought he would make an end of it. So he climbed up the side of the house and entered through the window.

At first he was very angry, but when he saw Pinocchio really stretched out on the floor without any feet, he felt sorry, and he took him gently by the neck and began to caress him. Swallowing a big sob, he said, "You dear little Pinocchio! How is it that you have burned off your feet?"

"I do not know, Papa; but, believe me, the night has been a horrible one, and I shall remember it always. It thundered and lightened and I was so very hungry! And the Talking Cricket said to me: 'It serves you right; you have been wicked and you deserve it all.' I said to him, 'Take care, Cricket'; and he said to me, 'You are a marionette and have a wooden head.' I then took a hammer and threw it at him and it killed him. Then I placed a saucepan on some burning shavings to cook an egg, but when I broke the egg a little chicken flew out of the shell and said, 'Good-by, little one.' Meanwhile I grew more hungry and ran to a house and rang the doorbell for help. An old man with his nightcap on came to the window and told me to go away. Was that a nice way to treat a boy? I came home at once and dropped into that chair and placed my feet on the stove. Now you have come back and found me with my feet all gone, and I am still very hungry. Ih! ih! ih! ih!

And poor Pinocchio began to cry so loudly that he could be heard for miles.

Geppetto, who, through all the sad story, thought of only one thing, and that was that the marionette was dying of hunger, suddenly pulled out of his pocket three pears and handing them to the marionette said: "These three pears were to have been my breakfast, but I give them to you willingly. Eat them, and may they do you good."

"If you want me to eat them, be so kind as to peel them."

"Peel them?" replied Geppetto, greatly surprised. "I would never have believed that you could be so hard to please. Bad boy! In this world little boys must eat what is given them."

"That is all right," said Pinocchio, "but I never eat fruit unless it is peeled. I cannot eat the skins."

And that good man Geppetto took out of his pocket a small knife and with much patience peeled the three pears and placed all the skins on the corner of the table.

After Pinocchio had eaten the first pear in two mouthfuls, he was in the act of throwing away the core, when Geppetto took him by the arms and said to him: "Do not throw the core away. Everything in this world has its use."

"But I never eat the core," cried the marionette, wriggling like a snake.

"All right!" said Geppetto, without getting angry.

The result was that the three cores, instead of being thrown away, were placed on the corner of the table with the skins.

Having eaten, or, to describe it more truly, having devoured, the three pears, Pinocchio gave a long yawn and said, "I am still hungry."

"But, my boy, I have nothing more to give you."

"Nothing more, truly?"

"Nothing, except those skins and cores."

"Oh, well," said Pinocchio, "if there is nothing more, I will eat the skins."

And he commenced to eat them. At first he puckered his mouth, but one after another the skins disappeared. After the skins he ate the cores also. When he had eaten everything he clapped his hands contentedly on his little stomach and said, "Now I feel better."

"You see now," said Geppetto, "that I was right when I told you that you must accustom yourself to what is given you and not be too dainty. My dear boy, no one ever knows what may happen in this world, so always be prepared for the worst."

CHAPTER VIII

The marionette had scarcely appeased his hunger when he began to grumble and cry because he wished a new pair of feet. Geppetto, in order to punish him for his bad actions, let him cry for half a day. Then he said: "And why should I make you a new pair of feet? Perhaps you would run away again."

"I promise you," said the marionette, sobbing, "that hereafter I will be a good boy."

"All boys," said Geppetto, "when they wish to obtain something, say that."

"I promise you that I will go to school. I will study and I will be an honor —"

"All boys, when they wish to obtain something, tell the same story."

29

"But I am not like other boys. I am better than all the rest and I always speak the truth. I promise you, Papa, that I will learn a trade, and that I will be your consolation and your support in your old age."

Geppetto, although he had the face of a tyrant, began to shed tears, and his heart was full of compassion when he saw poor little Pinocchio in such a state. He took his tools and two pieces of wood and began to work very diligently.

In less than an hour the new feet were finished. They were two nimble and nervous feet, and were made so beautifully that they looked as if they might have been carved by a great artist. Then Geppetto said to the marionette, "Close your eyes and go to sleep."

Pinocchio closed his eyes and pretended to sleep. Meantime Geppetto stuck on the two feet with a little glue; and he did it so well that one could hardly see the places where they were joined. As soon as the marionette saw that his feet were on, he jumped down and began to dance around as if he were mad with joy.

"In order to pay you back for your kindness," said Pinocchio to his papa, "I wish to go to school immediately."

"Good boy!"

"But in order to go to school I need some clothes."

Geppetto, who was so poor that he had not a cent in his pocket, made a beautiful suit of clothes out of some cardboard painted all over with flowers. He made a pair of shoes out of the bark of a tree, and a cap out of stale bread crumbs all molded together.

Pinocchio ran immediately to look at himself in a tub filled with water, and he was so delighted with his appearance that he said proudly, "Truly, I look like a gentleman!"

"Yes, indeed," replied Geppetto, "because, bear in mind, it is not fine clothes so much as clean ones that make a gentleman."

"By the by," added the marionette, "now in order to go to school I lack something else."

"What is that?"

"Why, I lack an A B C card."

"You are right; but how can I get one?"

"That is easy. Go to the store and buy it."

"And the money?"

"I have none."

"Neither have I," added the good old man, looking sad.

Pinocchio, although he was a happy boy, looked sad too, because real trouble is understood by everybody, even by boys.

"Have patience!" cried Geppetto, suddenly getting up. Taking off his coat all covered with patches, he ran out of the house.

After a little while he returned with an A B C card in his hand, but his coat was gone. The poor man was in his shirt sleeves and it was snowing outside too.

"And the coat, Papa?"

"I have sold it."

"Why did you sell it?"

"Because it made me too warm."

Pinocchio understood the reply at once, and not being able to restrain his feelings, he jumped up on Geppetto, threw his arms around his neck, and kissed his face all over.

CHAPTER IX

The snow having stopped, Pinocchio, with his
nice new A B C card under his arm, went to school.
As he walked along he imagined many things and
built a thousand castles in the air, each new one
more beautiful than the others. And, talking to
himself, he said: "To-day at school I wish to learn
immediately to read; to-morrow I will learn to
write, and then the day after to-morrow I will
learn to make numbers. Then with my learning I
will earn many pennies, and with the pennies that
will fill my pocket I will order my papa a nice new
suit of cloth. But why did I say of cloth? I will
have one of gold and line it with silver and have

buttons of brilliants. My poor papa deserves it truly, because in order to buy me an A B C card so that I could learn, he is now in his shirt sleeves, in the cold weather too! There are not many papas who would sacrifice so much."

While he was talking thus he seemed to hear some music of a fife and strokes of a drum — *pi-pi-pi, pi-pi-pi, zum, zum, zum, zùm*. He stopped to listen. These sounds came from the end of a long street that led to a small square near the sea. "What is that beautiful music? It is too bad that I have to go to school. If — " And he remained there perplexed. He must decide either to go to school or to hear the fife and drum. "To-day I will go and hear the fife and drum, and to-morrow I will go to school. There is always time to go there," said the little scoundrel, shrugging his shoulders.

No sooner said than done. He turned down the street and ran as hard as he could. The more he ran, the more distinct became the sound of the fife and drum — *pi-pi-pi, pi-pi-pi, pi-pi-pi, zum, zum, zum, zum*. He soon found himself in the middle of a square, which was filled with people. They all stood around a little wooden building with a sign painted in many colors.

"What is that house?" asked Pinocchio, turning to a boy standing near.

"Read the sign and you will know."

"I should be glad to read it, but somehow to-day I do not know how."

"Stupid one! then I will read it for you.   Know, then, that on that sign with letters like fire there is written, 'Grand Theater of Marionettes.'"

"How soon does it begin?"

"It begins now."

"And how much is the admission?"

"Four pennies."

Pinocchio was wild with curiosity, and forgetting all his good resolutions, shamelessly turned to the boy with whom he was talking and said, "Would you give me four pennies until to-morrow?"

"I would give you the pennies willingly, but to-day I have none to spare."

"For four pennies I will sell you my jacket," said the marionette.

"What good would a paper cardboard jacket do me?   If it rains on it, it will fall apart."

"I will sell my shoes."

"They are good only for a fire."

"How much will you give me for my cap?"

"Nice bargain, truly! a cap of bread!   Why, the rats would eat it all in a night."

Pinocchio was full of trouble.   He stood there not knowing what to do.   He had not the courage to offer the last thing he had.   He hesitated, but finally he said, "Will you give me four pennies for this A B C card?"

"I am a boy and I do not buy from boys," replied the little fellow, who had more good sense than the marionette.

"For four pennies I will take the A B C card," said a seller of old clothes, who heard the conversation.   So the card was sold at once.   And to think that the poor man, Geppetto, remained at home trembling in his shirt sleeves in the cold, just to buy that A B C card for his son!

CHAPTER X

When Pinocchio entered the theater of the marionettes something happened that almost caused a revolution.

The reader must know that the curtain was up and the comedy had begun. On the stage Harlequin and Pulcinello were quarreling, and, as usual in stage performances of marionettes, there were many blows given with a stick. The audience were listening intently. They laughed out loud on hearing the quarrel of the two marionettes, who gesticulated and acted their threats as naturally as if they had been two real people.

Suddenly Harlequin stopped reciting. Turning toward the audience and pointing to some one in the rear, he began to shout in a dramatic tone:

38

" What do my eyes behold ? do I dream or am I awake ? Nevertheless that boy there is Pinocchio."

" It is Pinocchio, truly ! " said Pulcinello.

" It is indeed he ! " screamed Rosa, who peeped from behind the scenes.

" It is Pinocchio ! It is Pinocchio ! " cried in a chorus all the marionettes, coming out and jumping on the stage.

" Pinocchio, come up here to me," cried Harlequin. " Come and throw your arms around your wooden brothers."

At this affecting invitation Pinocchio made a jump, and from the back part of the theater he went to the reserved portion ; then with another jump from the reserved seats he mounted on the head of the orchestra leader, and from there he jumped upon the stage.

It is impossible to imagine the kisses, the embraces, the words of endearment, the woodenheaded sayings of true and sincere brotherhood that Pinocchio received in the midst of the actors and actresses of that dramatic company. It was a touching sight ; but the public, seeing that the comedy was stopped, grew impatient and began to cry, " We want the play."

It was all breath thrown away, for the marionettes, instead of continuing the dialogue, redoubled their cries ; and taking Pinocchio on their shoulders, they carried him in triumph behind the wings on the stage.

Then came out the manager, a big man, who made people tremble just by looking at them. He had a beard, black as ink, which reached to his feet and tripped him when he walked. His mouth was as large as a furnace, his eyes looked like two lanterns of red glass, and in his hands he cracked a large whip made of serpents and tails of wolves tied together.

At the unexpected sight of the manager all the marionettes became mute. No one breathed. Why, you could have heard a fly walk! The poor marionettes, both actors and actresses, trembled like so many leaves.

"Why have you come here and made all this disorder in my theater?" he asked, looking at Pinocchio. His voice sounded like that of an ogre with a cold in his head.

"Believe me, most illustrious man, the fault is not mine!"

"Do not answer me! to-night we will settle our affairs."

The marionettes went on with the comedy and the manager went to the kitchen where he was preparing for supper a sheep that was cooking on a spit. As he needed more wood to finish cooking it, he called Harlequin and Pulcinello, who had finished their performance, and said to them: "Bring me now the marionette that you will find tied to a nail. He appears to be made of good dry wood, and I am sure he will make a beautiful flame for a roast."

Harlequin and Pulcinello at first hesitated, but a glance from their master's eye scared them and they obeyed. Soon they returned to the kitchen carrying Pinocchio in their arms. Struggling like an eel out of water, he cried despairingly: "Oh, Papa, dear Papa, save me! I do not wish to die! No, I do not wish to die!"

CHAPTER XI

The proprietor, Fire Eater (for that was his name), looked fearful with his black beard covering his chest and legs like an apron; but he really was not a bad man. When he saw Pinocchio carried before him and crying, "I do not want to die! I do not want to die!" he began to pity him. He resisted the feeling for a little while, but when he could do so no longer he gave a terrible sneeze.

At that sound Harlequin, who until then had been afflicted and doubled up like a weeping willow, began to look more lively, and leaning toward Pinocchio, whispered to him softly, "Good news, brother! Our master has sneezed. That is a sign that he pities you, and now you are saved."

For you must know that while many men and women cry when they feel moved to pity, Fire

Eater, instead, had the habit of sneezing. It was his way of letting others know the tenderness of his heart.

After having sneezed, the manager, still looking cross, cried to Pinocchio: "Stop crying! Your sobs distress me very much. I feel a spasm that nearly — *etchi-etchi* — " and he sneezed twice more.

"God bless you!" said Pinocchio.

"Thanks. And your papa and mamma are still living?" asked Fire Eater.

"My papa, yes; but I have never seen my mother."

"Oh, what a terrible thing it would have been for your papa if I had thrown you on the fire! Poor old man! I pity him — *etchi-etchi-etchi* — " and he sneezed three times more.

"God bless you!" said Pinocchio.

"Thanks. But some one must also pity me, because you see I have no more wood with which I can cook my meat; and you would have made a fine fire. But now that I am moved to pity for you, I must have patience. Instead of you I shall have to burn some one of my company. Ho! guards, come here!"

At this command two guards of wood appeared with soldier caps on their heads and swords by their

sides.   Then the manager said to them in a wheez-
ing tone : " Bring me Harlequin, bound tightly,
and then throw him on the fire.   I want that roast
cooked well."

Just imagine how poor Harlequin must have felt !
He was so scared that his legs refused to support
him, and he fell face downward on the floor.   Pinocchio, at this most pitiful sight, threw himself at
the feet of the manager, and, crying so hard that he
wet the long, black beard of Fire Eater, said in a
supplicating voice, " Pity, Mr. Fire Eater ! "

" There are no Misters here," replied the manager
in a dry tone.

" Pity, Mr. Cavalier ! "

" There are no cavaliers here."

" Pity, Mr. Commander ! "

" There are no commanders here."

" Pity, Your Excellency ! "

At hearing himself called " Excellency " the
manager immediately pursed up his lips and became
more humane and tractable.   He said to Pinocchio,
" Well, what do you wish ? "

" I ask pity for poor Harlequin."

" I have saved you, but I must put some one on
the fire, so that my meat shall be well cooked."

" In that case," cried Pinocchio, proudly, straightening himself and throwing aside his cap of bread

crumbs, — "in that case I know what my duty should be. Come, guards, bind me and throw me into the flames. No, it is not just that poor Harlequin, my true friend, should die for me!"

These words, pronounced in a loud tone and with heroic accents, made all the marionettes that were present at this scene cry. The guards, although made of wood, wept like two baby lambs.

Fire Eater at first remained hard and cold as a piece of ice; but afterward he slowly began to show symptoms of being moved and of sneezing. After having sneezed four or five times, he held out his arms to Pinocchio and said: "You are a brave boy. Come here and give me a kiss."

Pinocchio ran quickly, and, climbing like a squirrel up the beard of the manager, gave him a most beautiful kiss right on the point of his nose.

"Then I am free?" asked Harlequin, with a thin voice that could scarcely be heard.

"Yes, you are free," replied Fire Eater. Then he added, sighing and shaking his head: "To-night I will eat my supper half-cooked; but another time, woe to him who changes my plans!"

When the marionettes heard that Harlequin was free they ran to the stage, lit all the lights, just as if it were a grand holiday, and began to dance and jump. And they danced all night long.

CHAPTER XII

The next morning Fire Eater called Pinocchio aside and said to him, " What is your papa's name?"

" Geppetto."

" What is his business?"

" He is poor."

" Does he earn much?"

" He earns so much that he never has a cent in his pockets. Just imagine, in order to buy me an A B C card he had to sell his coat! It was covered with patches, but they gave him enough so that he could buy me that."

" Poor man! I pity him very much. Here are five pieces of gold. Go quickly and carry them to him, and remember me kindly to him."

Pinocchio, as it is easy to imagine, thanked the manager many times. He embraced the marionettes one after another, and, now nearly crazy with joy, started to go home. But he had not gone half a mile when he met a Fox lame in one paw, and a Cat blind in both eyes. The Fox, who limped, leaned on the Cat; and the Cat, who was blind, was guided by the Fox.

"Good morning, Pinocchio," said the Fox, saluting him politely.

"How do you know my name?" asked the marionette.

"I know your papa very well."

"When did you see him?"

"I saw him yesterday at the door of his house."

"What was he doing?"

"He was in his shirt sleeves and he trembled with the cold."

"Poor Papa! but he will tremble no more after to-day."

"Why?"

"Because I have become a great, rich man."

"You a great, rich man!" said the Fox, and he laughed aloud. The Cat also laughed, but in order not to be seen laughing he stroked his mustache with his two front paws.

"What are you laughing about?" said Pinocchio,

taken aback. "I hate to make your mouths water, but I have here, as you shall see, five beautiful pieces of gold."

And he pulled out of his pocket the money that Fire Eater had given him. At the sound of the money the Fox involuntarily stretched his leg that was paralyzed and the Cat opened wide his eyes that looked like two green lamps; but it was all done so quickly that Pinocchio did not see anything.

"And now," said the Fox, "what do you intend to do with all that money?"

"First of all," replied the marionette, "I shall buy a coat for my papa, all covered with gold and silver and with buttons of brilliants. Then I shall buy a new A B C card for myself."

"For yourself?"

"Yes, indeed, because I wish to go to school and begin to study."

"Look at me!" said the Fox; "because of my passion for studying I have lost a leg."

"Look at me!" cried the Cat; "because of my love for studying I have lost both eyes."

In the meantime a Blackbird flew near them and said: "Pinocchio, do not listen to the counsel of bad companions. If you do, you will be sorry."

Just as soon as the Blackbird had said that, the Cat gave a spring and caught him by the back.

Before the Blackbird had time to say "Oh!" the Cat ate him up, feathers and all. Then the Cat cleaned his mouth and closed his eyes and became as blind as he was at first.

"Poor Blackbird!" said Pinocchio. "Why did you treat him so badly?"

"I did it to teach him a lesson. Another time he will know that he ought not to meddle with other people's business."

They walked along a short distance when the Fox, stopping suddenly, said to the marionette, "Should you like to double your money?"

"What do you mean?"

"Should you like to make of those miserable five pieces, ten? a hundred? a thousand?"

"Why, of course! And how can you do it?"

"It is very easy. Instead of going home, come with us."

"And where do you want to take me?"

"To the Country of the Owl."

Pinocchio thought a little and then said resolutely: "No, I will not go. My father expects me. Who knows but that the poor old man, when I did not return yesterday, was worried and wept for me? I have been a bad boy, and the Talking Cricket was right when he said, 'Disobedient boys never get along well in this world.' I have had one experience because I was bad. Only last night, at the house of Fire Eater, I was in great danger. *Brrr!* It makes me tremble to think of it."

"Then," said the Fox, "you want to go home? All right! Go home, but it will be the worse for you."

"Yes, it will be the worse for you," said the Cat.

"Think well, Pinocchio, for you have thrown away a fortune."

"A fortune," said the Cat.

"Your five pieces might be two thousand by to-morrow."

"Two thousand," repeated the Cat.

"But how is it possible that they can become so many?" asked Pinocchio, whose mouth was wide open with astonishment.

"I will explain to you," said the Fox. "You must know that in the Country of the Owl there is a magic field called 'The Field of Wonders.' You make a little hole in the ground and you put inside, for example, one piece of gold. Then you cover over the hole with a little earth, water it with a few drops of water from a fountain, put on a little salt, and go to bed and sleep quietly. In the meantime, during the night, the gold piece begins to grow and blossom; and the next morning, returning to the field, guess what you find? Why, you find a tree loaded with gold pieces!"

"If I bury five pieces," said Pinocchio, all excited, "how many shall I find next morning?"

"It is easy to count," replied the Fox. "You can do it on your fingers. Every gold piece will make five hundred; and therefore, multiplying each by five, you will have two thousand five hundred."

"Oh, how beautiful!" cried Pinocchio, dancing with joy. "When I have all those gold pieces I will give you five hundred of them and I will take the other two thousand to my papa."

"A present to us!" cried the Fox, disdainfully, as if he were offended. "No, indeed!"

"No, indeed!" said the Cat.

"We," said the Fox, "work only to enrich others."

"Only others," said the Cat.

"What good people!" thought Pinocchio; and forgetting all about his papa, the new coat, and the A B C card, he said to the Fox and the Cat, "Come on, then; I will go with you."

CHAPTER XIII

They walked and walked and walked until they arrived at the Red Lobster Inn, tired to death.

"Let us stop here a little," said the Fox, "just long enough to get something to eat and rest ourselves. At midnight we can start again and to-morrow morning we shall arrive at the Field of Wonders."

They entered the inn and seated themselves at the table, but none of them was hungry. The poor Cat felt very much indisposed and could eat only thirty-five mullets with tomato sauce and four portions of tripe; and because the tripe did not taste just right he called three times for butter and cheese to put on it.

The Fox would willingly have ordered something, but as the doctor had told him to diet, he had to be contented with a nice fresh rabbit dressed with the giblets of chicken. After the rabbit he ordered, as a finish to his meal, some partridges, some pheasants, some frogs, some lizards, and some bird of paradise eggs; and then he did not wish any more. He had such a distaste for food, he said, that he could not eat another mouthful.

Pinocchio ate the least of all. He asked for a piece of meat and some bread, but he left everything on his plate. He could think of nothing but the Field of Wonders.

When they had supped the Fox said to the host: "Give me two good rooms, one for Mr. Pinocchio and another for me and my companion. Before we go we will ring the bell. Remember, however, to wake us at midnight so that we can go on with our journey."

"All right, sir," replied the host; and he winked his eye at the Fox and the Cat, as if to say, "We understand each other."

Pinocchio had scarcely jumped into bed when he fell asleep and began to dream. He seemed to be in a field full of arbors, and each arbor was overgrown with vines covered with large bunches of grapes. Instead of grapes, however, they were all

gold pieces, that made a noise when the wind blew —*zin-zin-zin-zin.* It was just as if they said, "Here we are! Let who will come and take us." When Pinocchio was on the point of reaching for them he heard a loud knocking at the door of his room. It was the landlord who came to tell him that the clock had struck midnight.

"And are my companions ready?" asked the marionette.

"Better than that! They left two hours ago."

"Why were they in such a hurry?"

"Because the Cat received word that his father was very sick with frosted feet and that he was in danger of losing his life."

"And they paid for the supper?"

"What do you think those people are? They are too highly educated to insult a gentleman as good as you are."

"Oh, yes! That affront would have displeased me very much," said Pinocchio, hastily. Then he asked the landlord, "Did they say where I should meet them?"

"At the Field of Wonders, to-morrow morning at daybreak."

Pinocchio paid a gold piece for his supper and that of his companions, and then departed. He groped his way along, because outside the inn it was so dark that he could not see anything. It was very quiet and not even a leaf stirred. Some birds flying along the road struck Pinocchio on the nose with their wings. He jumped back and cried out with fear, "Who goes there?" The echo of the surrounding hills took up his words and repeated, "Who

goes there?" "Who goes there?" "Who goes there?"

As he walked on, he saw on the trunk of a tree a little creature that shone with a pale opaque light, just like a candle behind a globe of transparent porcelain.

"Who are you?" asked Pinocchio.

"I am the Spirit of the Talking Cricket," it replied, with a little voice that seemed to come from another world.

" What do you want with me ? "

" I wish to warn you. Go back, with your four gold pieces that you have left, to your papa, who cries and thinks he shall never see you again."

" To-morrow my papa will be a very rich man, because these four pieces will become two thousand."

" Do not trust those who promise to make you rich in one night, my boy. Usually they are mad or deceitful. Listen to me and go back."

" I want to go on."

" The hour is late."

" I want to go on."

" The night is dark."

" I want to go on."

" The road is dangerous."

" I want to go on."

" Remember that boys who always do what they want to will sooner or later repent."

" The same old story ! Good night, Cricket."

" Good night, and may you escape from the assassins ! "

The Talking Cricket had hardly said these words when he suddenly disappeared, just as if some one had blown the light out, and the road was darker than ever.

CHAPTER XIV

"Truly," said the marionette to himself, starting again on his way, "how unfortunate we poor boys are! Everybody scolds us, everybody warns us, and everybody gives us advice. Why, everybody takes it upon himself to be our papa and master,— even the Talking Cricket. Here am I; and because I would not pay attention to that tiresome Talking Cricket, he said that many things would happen to me! I should also meet assassins! I have never believed in assassins. I think that assassins have been invented by papas on purpose to make their boys afraid to go out at night. And then, if I should meet them on the road, they would probably tell me my way. Why, I am not afraid. I would go to them and say, right to their faces, 'Mr. Assassins, what do you want of me? Do not think that you can fool with me. Go away then about your own business, quick!' At such talk the poor assassins — I can see them now — would run away like the wind. In case they might be clever enough not to run away, why then I would — and thus the thing would end — "

But Pinocchio was not able to finish his reasoning, because at that moment he thought he heard a rustling in the leaves behind him. He turned to look and saw in the dark two coal sacks covering two figures which ran toward him on the tips of their toes like ghosts.

"Here they are, truly!" said Pinocchio to himself. Not knowing what to do with the four gold pieces, he put them into his mouth and under his tongue. Then he tried to run away. But he had hardly started when his arms were seized and he heard two hollow voices say to him, "Your money or your life!"

Not being able to reply on account of the money in his mouth, Pinocchio made many bows and gestures in order to make his captors understand that he was a poor marionette and that he did not have a cent in his pockets. "Come on and stop fooling! Out with it!" the brigands cried. And the marionette made signs with his hands and head, which meant, "I have none!"

"Bring out the money or you will die!" said the taller assassin.

"You will die," repeated the smaller one.

"And after you are dead we will kill your papa."

"We will kill your papa," repeated the other.

"No, no, no! Not my poor papa!" cried Pinocchio, despairingly ; but in saying this the gold pieces made a noise in his mouth.

"Oh, you story-teller! you have hidden the money in your mouth! Out with it!"

Poor Pinocchio remained quiet.

"Ah! do you make believe you are deaf? Wait a little and we will show you how we shall make you give up the gold."

Then they began to handle the marionette very roughly, but Pinocchio managed to liberate himself from their hands. Jumping a hedge that bordered the road, he began to run across the fields with the assassins after him, like two dogs after a rabbit.

After a run of fifteen miles Pinocchio could go no farther. Fearing that he was lost, he climbed to the top of a large pine tree and sat on one of the branches. The assassins also tried to climb;

but when they got halfway up they slipped and fell to the ground, rubbing the skin off their legs and hands as they dropped.

However, they did not consider themselves conquered. On the contrary, they collected a bundle of sticks, and placing them around the tree, set fire

to them. In less time than it takes to tell it, the pine tree took fire and blazed like a candle blown by the wind. Pinocchio, seeing that the flames mounted higher and higher, and not wishing to be roasted, jumped down from the top of the tree. Away he ran, just as before, with the assassins always behind and never getting tired.

Meanwhile the day dawned and they found themselves on the edge of a large trench filled with dirty water, just the color of coffee and cream. What could they do? " One, two, three," said Pinocchio; and bending down and making a great spring, he landed safely on the other side. The assassins jumped also, but they did not take the right measure; and splash! they both fell into the trench. Pinocchio, who heard the plunge and the splash, cried out, " I hope you had a nice bath, Mr. Assassins!" and then began to run again. He thought that they were drowned; but looking back, he saw them running as before, the water dripping from their wet clothes as they followed him.

CHAPTER XV

Then the marionette, losing his courage, was on
the point of throwing himself on the ground and
giving himself up as conquered, when, looking
around, he saw in the middle of a dark forest,
shining afar, a little house as white as snow. "If
I have enough breath to reach that house, perhaps
I shall be saved," he said to himself. And without
delaying a minute, he began to run through the
forest as fast as he could. The assassins still
followed him.

Finally, after a desperate run of two hours, he
arrived, out of breath, at the door of the house
and knocked. No one replied. He knocked again
with great force because he heard approaching

the steps and heavy breathing of his pursuers. The same silence.

Seeing that the knocking did not have any effect, he began to kick and beat the door in desperation. Then there appeared at the door a beautiful Fairy with blue hair. Her hands were crossed on her breast. When she saw Pinocchio she said, "In this house there is no one; they have all gone away."

"Open the door at least for me, won't you?" cried Pinocchio, weeping.

"I am also waiting to go away."

Scarcely had she said this when the Fairy disappeared and the window closed without making any noise.

"Oh, beautiful Fairy with the Blue Hair," cried Pinocchio, "open the door, for goodness' sake! Have compassion on a poor boy followed by assass—" But he could not finish the word because he felt himself seized by the neck. Then he heard the voices of his captors scolding him and crying, "Now you cannot run away from us again."

The marionette, seeing death staring him in the face, trembled so that all his joints made a great noise and the four gold pieces jingled in his mouth.

"Now," said the assassins, "will you open your mouth? Yes or no? Ah, you do not reply? All right! This time we will open it!" And they took two knives, sharp as razors, and — *zaff-zaff* — they gave him two strokes in the middle of the back.

Fortunately the marionette was made of good hard wood. The blades of the knives broke into several pieces and the assassins were left looking at each other, with only the handles of the knives in their hands.

"I understand," said one of them. "We must hang him. Let us hang him, then."

"Let us hang him," said the other.

No sooner said than done. They bound his hands and hanged him to a branch of a tree

called the Grand Oak. Then they sat down on the ground to wait until the marionette should die. After three hours, however, the marionette's eyes were still open and his mouth was closed, and he kicked harder than ever.

Finally, annoyed by this long delay, they turned to Pinocchio and said to him, laughing aloud: "Good-by until to-morrow morning! When we return here we hope that you will be polite enough to die and have your mouth opened wide." And they went away.

Meanwhile a great wind began to blow Pinocchio backward and forward, just like a large bell. Although he felt death approaching, yet he hoped every moment that some one would come and save him. But when he found that no one would help him he remembered his poor papa and stammered, "Oh, my Papa, if you were only here now!" But he had no breath to say any more.

CHAPTER XVI

While poor Pinocchio hung from the branch of the Grand Oak and appeared more dead than alive, the beautiful Fairy with the Blue Hair came to the window. Pitying the poor unfortunate who was swinging backward and forward, she clapped her hands three times. At this signal the beating of wings was heard and a great Falcon came and placed himself on the window sill.

"What do you command, my gracious Fairy?" said the Falcon, lowering his beak in a bow of reverence. For you must know that the Fairy with the Blue Hair was none other than a beautiful enchantress, who for more than a thousand years had lived in the neighborhood of this forest.

"Do you see that marionette hanging on yonder Grand Oak?"

"I see him."

"Fly quickly there and untie with your strong beak the knot that holds him suspended and lay him gently on the ground."

The Falcon flew away and after two minutes returned, saying, "That which you have commanded is done."

"How did you find him — alive or dead?"

"He appeared to be dead, but he cannot really be so. Scarcely had I untied the knot and laid him gently on the ground when he gave a sigh and said, 'Now I feel better.'"

Then the Fairy clapped her hands twice and a Bearded Dog appeared, walking on his hind legs, just like a man. The Bearded Dog was dressed in livery. He had a cap trimmed with gold lace and a white curly wig that came down to his neck. He wore a dress coat of chocolate color, with buttons of brilliants and two big pockets to hold bones. He had a pair of short boots of crimson velvet and he carried behind him a sort of umbrella cover in which he put his tail when it rained.

" My brave Fido," said the Fairy to the Bearded Dog, " go quickly, hitch up the most beautiful carriage in my stables and take the road to the forest. When you arrive under the Grand Oak you will find stretched out on the ground a poor marionette, half dead. Take him up carefully and bring him here. Do you understand ? "

The Bearded Dog, in order to show that he understood, shook the cover to his tail three or four times and departed in a flash. A little while afterward a beautiful transparent carriage, all trimmed with canary-bird feathers and lined inside with cream-colored cloth, was seen to come from the stables. It was drawn by one hundred pairs of white mice and the Bearded Dog sat on the box and cracked his whip from right to left as a coachman always does when he fears he shall be late.

A quarter of an hour had hardly passed when the carriage returned. The Fairy, who waited at the door, took the marionette in her arms and carried him to a little bed of mother-of-pearl, which she had prepared for him. Then she sent immediately for three doctors. They soon arrived, one after the other. They were a Crow, an Owl, and a Talking Cricket.

" I should like to know from you, gentlemen," said the Fairy, turning to the three doctors who

surrounded the bed of Pinocchio, — "I should like to know if this unhappy marionette is dead or alive."

At this invitation the Crow stepped forward, tested the pulse of Pinocchio, tested his nose, and then his little toe. When he had tested him thoroughly he pronounced these words: "It is my

belief that the marionette is quite dead; but if through some awkwardness he should not be dead, then it would be a sure sign that he is alive."

"It pains me," said the Owl, "to have to contradict the Crow, my illustrious friend and colleague. To me, however, the marionette is quite alive; but if through some awkwardness he should not be alive, then it would be a sure sign that he is dead."

"And have you nothing to say?" said the Fairy to the Talking Cricket.

"I say that a prudent doctor should be quiet when he does not know what to say. Besides, that marionette has a familiar face. I know him a little."

Pinocchio, who until then had been as immovable as a piece of wood, began to tremble so violently that he shook the bed.

"That marionette," continued the Talking Cricket, "is a good for nothing."

Pinocchio opened his eyes and then closed them suddenly.

"He is a scamp, a rogue, a vagabond."

Pinocchio hid his face under the covers.

"That marionette is a disobedient child who is killing his poor papa."

At this point crying and sobbing were heard in the room. Imagine how surprised everybody was when the covers were pulled down and the crying and sobbing were found to come from Pinocchio!

"When the dead cry," said the Crow, "it is a sign that they are on the road to recovery."

"It grieves me to contradict my illustrious friend and colleague," added the Owl, "but to my mind, when the dead cry it is a sign that they do not want to die."

CHAPTER XVII

Scarcely had the three doctors left the room
when the Fairy approached Pinocchio, and after
touching his forehead perceived that he had taken
a fever of not saying anything.

Then she put a little bit of white powder in a
glass of water and, handing it to the marionette,
said to him sweetly, "Drink, and in a few days
you will be cured." Pinocchio looked at the glass,
made a mouth, then with a voice full of sobs said,
"Is it sweet or bitter?"

"It is bitter, but it will do you good."

"If it is bitter, I do not want it."

"Listen to me; drink it."

"I do not like bitter things."

"Drink it; and when you have drunk it I will
give you a little ball of sugar to take the taste out
of your mouth."

"Where is the ball of sugar?"

"Here it is," said the Fairy, taking out a ball of sugar.

"First I want the ball of sugar; then I will drink the bitter water."

"You promise me?"

"Yes."

The Fairy gave him the sugar, and Pinocchio, after having crushed it to atoms, said, licking his lips, "How nice! If sugar could only be medicine, I would take it all day long."

"Now keep your promise and drink these few bitter drops. They will cure you."

Pinocchio unwillingly took the glass in his hand and put it under his nose; then he put it to his lips; then he put it under his nose again. Finally he said: "It is too bitter! It is too bitter! I cannot drink it."

"How can you say that when you have not tasted it?"

"I know. I smell it. I want another ball of sugar first; then I will drink it."

So the Fairy, with the patience of an indulgent mamma, placed in his mouth another ball of sugar and then gave him the glass again. "I cannot drink it," said the marionette, making numerous grimaces.

"Why?"

"Because that pillow on my feet annoys me."

The Fairy took the pillow away.

"It is useless, I cannot drink it even now."

"What troubles you now?"

"That door is half open."

The Fairy went and closed the door.

"Really," cried Pinocchio, breaking forth into tears, "I cannot drink that bitter water! No, no, no!"

"My child, you will be sorry."

"I do not care."

"Your fever is bad."

"I do not care."

"The fever will carry you in a few hours to another world."

"I do not care."

"Have you no fear of death?"

"No. I have no fear. I would rather die than take that bad medicine."

Just at that moment the door of the room opened and four Rabbits, black as ink, entered, carrying on their shoulders a coffin. "What do you want with

me?" cried Pinocchio, straightening himself up in his bed.

"We have come to take you away," replied the largest Rabbit.

"To take me away? But I am not dead!"

"Not now, no; but you have only a few more moments of life, having refused to drink the medicine that would cure your fever."

"Oh, my Fairy! oh, my Fairy!" screamed the marionette; "give me the glass quickly. Send them away; for I do not wish to die." And he took the glass in both hands and swallowed the medicine at one gulp.

"Oh, pshaw!" said the Rabbits; "we have made this trip for nothing." And placing the coffin on their shoulders again, the Rabbits went out of the room grumbling and muttering between their teeth.

The fact was that a few moments later Pinocchio jumped down from the bed well and strong; for you must know that wooden marionettes have the advantage of rarely being sick, and when they are they get well quickly. The Fairy, seeing him run through the room as lively and bright as a little chicken just out of its shell, said to him, "Then my medicine has cured you?"

"Yes, indeed! It has brought me back to this world."

"Then why was it that you begged me not to make you drink it?"

"Boys always behave so. We have more fear of the medicine than of the sickness."

"Shame on you! Boys ought to know that a good medicine taken in time may save them from serious trouble and perhaps from death."

"Oh! another time I will not behave so badly. I will remember the black Rabbits with the coffin on their shoulders and then I will take the medicine quickly."

"Now come here and tell me how it happened that you fell into the hands of assassins."

"Well, it happened in this way. The manager of the marionettes, Fire Eater, gave me five pieces of gold and said to me, 'Take these to your poor papa.' I met on the road a Fox and a Cat, two very nice persons, who said to me: 'Do you wish those pieces to become two thousand? Come with us and we will take you to the Field of Wonders.' I said, 'Let us go'; and they said, 'Let us stop at the Red Lobster Inn, and after midnight we will continue our journey.' When I awoke I found that they had gone. I then began to walk alone in the dark and I met two coal sacks with assassins inside who said to me, 'Give us your money.' I said, 'I have none'; I hid the gold pieces in my mouth.

One of the assassins tried to make me open my mouth, but I ran away as fast as I could across the fields. I climbed a tree, but they set fire to it and forced me to take to my heels again. The assassins ran after me until they caught me. They hanged me to a tree, and said, 'To-morrow we will come back, and then you will be dead and we can open your mouth. Then we shall be able to get the gold that is hidden under your tongue.'"

"And where have you put the four pieces of gold now?" asked the Fairy.

"I have lost them," replied Pinocchio. But he told a lie; for he had them in his pocket.

Scarcely had he told this lie when his nose, which was already long, grew two fingers longer.

"And where did you lose them?"

"In the forest."

At this second lie his nose grew still longer.

"If you have lost them in the forest, we will look for them and find them, because all that is lost in my forest is always found again."

" Oh, now I remember well," replied Pinocchio ; "the four pieces of money were swallowed when I took that medicine."

At this third lie the nose grew so long that poor Pinocchio could not turn himself round in the room. If he turned to one side, it struck the bed or the glass in the window ; if he turned to the other side, it struck the walls or the door of the room ; if he raised his head, he ran the risk of putting out one of the Fairy's eyes.

And the Fairy looked and laughed.

"Why do you laugh?" asked the marionette, quite confused and surprised because his nose had grown so long.

" I laugh at the foolish lies you have told."

" How do you know that I have told lies?"

" Lies, my boy, are recognized immediately, because there are two kinds : there are lies that have short legs and lies that have long noses. Yours seem to have long noses."

Pinocchio, not knowing where to hide himself for shame, tried to get out of the room, but he did not succeed. His nose had grown so large that he could not go through the door.

CHAPTER XVIII

What do you think? The Fairy let the marionette cry and weep for a good half hour because he could not go through the door on account of the length of his nose. She did this because she wished to teach him a lesson and show him how naughty he had been. But when she saw him so disfigured, his eyes nearly out of his head with desperation, she was moved to pity and struck her hands together. At that signal about a thousand birds called Woodpeckers flew into the room and, placing themselves on Pinocchio's nose, picked at it so hard that in a few minutes it was reduced to its usual size.

"How good you are, my Fairy!" said the marionette, drying his eyes, "and how I like you!"

"I like you too," replied the Fairy, "and if you will remain with me, you shall be my little brother and I will be your little sister."

"I will stay willingly — but my poor papa!"

"I have thought of everything; your father has been told already and before night he will be here."

"Truly?" cried Pinocchio, jumping with joy. "Then, my Fairy, if you are willing, I should like to go to meet him. I cannot wait to kiss that good old man, who has suffered so much for me."

"Go, but do not lose your way. Take the road to the forest and I am sure you will find him."

Pinocchio departed. As soon as he entered the forest he began to run like a deer. But when he arrived at a certain point, nearly in front of the Grand Oak, he stopped because he thought he heard some one. Indeed, he saw on the road — whom, do you suppose? — the Fox and the Cat, that

is, the two companions with whom he supped at the inn called the Red Lobster.

"Here is our dear friend Pinocchio!" cried the Fox, hugging and kissing him. "How did you ever get here?"

"How did you ever get here?" repeated the Cat.

"It is a long story," said the marionette, "and I will tell you when I have time. You know the night when you left me alone at the inn I met some assassins on the road."

"Assassins? Oh, my poor friend! and what did they want?"

"They wished to rob me of my money."

"Infamous!" said the Fox.

"Most infamous!" said the Cat.

"But I started to run," continued the marionette, "and they ran after me until they caught me and hanged me to a branch of that large oak." And Pinocchio pointed to the Grand Oak that was not far away.

"One could not imagine anything worse," said the Fox. "In what a world are we condemned to live! And now what are you doing here?"

"I am waiting for my papa, who may arrive at any moment."

"And your money, where is that?"

" I have it all, less the piece I spent at the inn called the Red Lobster."

" And to think that instead of four pieces they might become two thousand by to-morrow! Why did you not follow my advice? Why do you not sow them in the Field of Wonders?"

" To-day it is impossible. I will go another time."

" Another time will be too late," said the Fox.

" Why?"

" Because that field has been bought by a rich man, and after to-morrow no one will be permitted to sow there any more."

" How far is the Field of Wonders from here?"

" Hardly two miles. Will you come with us? In half an hour we shall be there. You can sow the money quickly, and after a few moments you can return home with your pockets full. Will you come with us?"

Pinocchio hesitated a little because he thought of the good Fairy, of old Geppetto, and of the advice of the Talking Cricket; but, after the fashion of foolish, heartless boys, he finally yielded. With a shake of his head he said to the Fox and the Cat, " Come on, I will go with you." And they started.

After having walked half a day they arrived at a city called Stupid-catchers. As soon as they entered the city Pinocchio saw all the streets full of sick dogs that gaped for food; clipped sheep that shook from the cold; featherless chickens that begged for alms; big butterflies that could not fly

any more because they had sold their beautiful wings for a few pennies and were ashamed to be seen; and pheasants that limped, bewailing their brilliant gold and silver feathers now lost to them forever.

In the midst of the crowd of beggars and un-
fortunates they passed from time to time several
fine carriages filled with people, each of whom
turned out to be a Fox or a thieving Magpie or a
Bird of Prey.

"Where is the Field of Wonders?" asked
Pinocchio.

"Only a few steps farther."

And so it proved. They walked through the
city, and outside the walls they stopped in a field
which looked much like other fields. No one was
in sight.

"Here we are at last," said the Fox. "Now
you must stoop down and dig a hole and put the
money inside."

Pinocchio obeyed, dug a hole, put in the money,
and then covered it over with earth.

"Now then," said the Fox, "go to that well and
take a little water and sprinkle the ground where
you have sown."

Pinocchio went to the well. Because he had
nothing in which to carry water, he took his shoe
and, filling it, came back and sprinkled the spot
where he had sown the money. Then he asked,
"Is there anything else?"

"Nothing else," replied the Fox. "Now we shall
go away. You may return here in about twenty

minutes and you will find a large vine with its
branches covered with money."

The poor marionette, nearly crazy with joy,
thanked the Fox and the Cat a thousand times
and promised them a beautiful present.

"We wish nothing," they replied. "To us it is
enough to have taught others the way to get rich
without doing anything; and we are as contented
as we can be."

Thus saying, they bowed to Pinocchio and, wishing him a good harvest, went away.

CHAPTER XIX

The marionette, returning to the city, began to count the minutes one by one. When he thought it was time to go back he took the road that led to the Field of Wonders. And while he walked along his heart beat in his bosom like a big hall clock — *tic-tac-tic-tac*. Meanwhile he was thinking to himself: "And if, instead of two thousand, I should find five thousand? Oh, what a rich man I should be! I would have a palace and a thousand wooden horses and carriages to amuse me; I would have a cellar filled with good things, a library filled with candy, Dutch cake, almond cake, and cinnamon stick."

Thus imagining, he arrived at the field. He stopped to look for the large vine with many branches, but he saw nothing. He took a few steps more. Nothing. He entered the field and went right to the hole where he had planted his money. There was nothing there. Then he became thoughtful and began to wonder what he should do next.

Just then he heard a whistling in his ears as if some one were laughing. Looking up, he saw on a tree a big Parrot who was preening his feathers.

"Why do you laugh?" asked Pinocchio in an angry voice.

"I laugh because in cleaning my feathers I tickled myself under my wings."

The marionette did not reply. He went to the well and sprinkled again the place where he had buried his money. When he had done this he heard a laugh more impertinent than the first one. It sounded very loud in the solitude of the field.

"Well," said Pinocchio, wrathfully, "tell me, if you can, ignorant Parrot, why you laugh now."

"I laugh at those silly heads who believe everything that is told them."

"Do you refer to me?"

"Yes, I speak of you, poor Pinocchio. You are foolish enough to think that money, if sowed properly, will grow like grain and plants. I thought so once, and in consequence I have to-day very few feathers. Now that it is too late to mend matters, I have made up my mind that in order to get together a few pennies it is necessary to work with your hands or invent something with your head."

"I do not understand," said the marionette, who already began to tremble with fear.

"I will explain better," said the Parrot. "Know, then, that while you were in the city the Fox and the Cat returned here. They took the money and then fled like the wind. And now they cannot be caught."

Pinocchio remained with his mouth wide open. Unwilling to believe the words of the Parrot, he began with his hands and nails to dig out the dirt where he had planted his money. And he dug and dug and dug until he had made a hole large enough for a haystack; but the money was not there.

In desperation he returned to the town. There he went before the tribunal and denounced the highwaymen who had stolen his money.

The judge was a Monkey of the race of Gorilla. He was old and looked respectable on account of his white beard, and especially so on account of his gold eyeglasses with no glass in them. These he wore all the time because of a weakness of the eyes, which had troubled him for many years.

Pinocchio told the judge everything; gave the names and addresses of the highwaymen, and finished by asking for justice.

The judge listened with much dignity. He took a lively interest in the story and seemed quite moved. When the marionette had no more to say,

the judge stretched out his hand and rang the bell. At that sound two large mastiff dogs entered, dressed like soldiers. Then the judge, pointing to Pinocchio, said to them: "This poor idiot has had his money stolen. Take him and put him in prison."

The marionette, hearing this sentence, began to protest; but the mastiffs, not wishing to waste time, covered his mouth and led him to a cell.

And there he remained four months and would have been there much longer if something fortunate had not happened. You must know, little readers, that the young emperor of the city called Stupid-catchers had just won a brilliant victory over his enemies. So he ordered a grand festival, fireworks and all sorts of parades, and to further celebrate his victory he opened all the prisons and liberated the convicts.

"If the other prisoners go out, I must go out too," said Pinocchio to the guard.

"You?" replied the guard; "no, because you are not a convict."

"Excuse me," replied Pinocchio, "I am as bad as any of them."

"In that case you are right," said the guard; and raising his hat respectfully and saluting him, he opened the door of his cell and allowed him to escape.

CHAPTER XX

Just imagine how happy Pinocchio was when he felt himself free! It is impossible to tell it. He quickly left the city and took the road that led to the house of the Fairy.

The roads were all soft because it had rained, and at every step he went up to his knees in mud. But he did not let that stop him. Wild with longing to see again his papa and his dear little sister with the blue hair, he ran and jumped on the dry places like a hare, and in running he splashed the mud all over his clothes and hat.

While he went along he thought: "How unfortunate I have been! But I deserve it all, because

I am a headstrong and touchy marionette. I always wish to do things my way, without paying any attention to those who love me and who are a thousand times wiser than I. But from now on I will change my life and become a good, obedient boy. I have found out that boys who are disobedient always lose in the long run. And my poor papa has waited for me so long! I shall find him at the house of the Fairy. It is so long since I have seen him that I will give him a thousand hugs and kisses. And the Fairy will pardon my naughtiness in going away. To think that I have received from her so much goodness and kindness! And to think also that I owe my life to her! But no one can be more thankful than I am."

He had scarcely said this last word when he stopped suddenly, very much frightened, and took four steps backward. What do you think he saw? — a big Serpent stretched out on the road! It had a green skin, eyes of fire, and a tail that smoked at the end just like a chimney!

It is impossible to imagine the fear of the marionette, who, going some distance away, sat down on a heap of stones and waited for the Serpent to go away so that the road would be left free. He waited one hour, two hours, three hours; but the Serpent did not move. Pinocchio could see nothing but the eyes of fire and the smoking tail. Then, screwing up his courage, the marionette approached within a few paces of the Serpent and said in a kind, sweet voice: "Excuse me, Mr. Serpent; would you oblige me by moving to one side so that I can pass?" It was as if he talked to a wall. There was no response.

Then Pinocchio said in the same kind tone: "You must know, Mr. Serpent, that I am going home, where my papa is waiting for me. Are you willing that I should pass and go on my way?"

He waited for some sign of response, but the reply did not come. On the contrary, the Serpent, which until then had been quite lively, became quiet and nearly benumbed. His eyes closed and his tail stopped smoking.

"He is dead, truly," thought Pinocchio, rubbing his hands with satisfaction. Without waiting any longer, he started to jump over him so as to pass to the other side. But he had hardly lifted his leg when the Serpent rose suddenly, like a spring let loose. The marionette, trying to jump back, tripped and fell to the ground with such force that he landed with his head half stuck in the mud and his feet in the air.

At the sight of the marionette kicking his legs with incredible velocity the Serpent was seized with convulsions of laughter. He laughed and laughed and laughed with such force that he broke a blood vessel and died.

Then Pinocchio started again to run along the road, hoping to reach the house of the Fairy before dark. Along the way, however, he was overcome

by hunger. So he jumped into a field to see if he could find a bunch of grapes. Here, too, he was unfortunate.

As soon as he arrived under the vine — *crac* — he felt his legs caught by two pieces of iron that made him see several new stars in the heavens. The poor marionette found himself fast in a trap which had been placed there by a farmer in order to catch a thieving Weasel of the neighborhood.

CHAPTER XXI

Pinocchio, you may well believe, began to cry and scream; but it was useless because there was not a house near him and no one passed along the road. In the meantime night came on. The trap hurt him so much, and he was so afraid of the dark, that he nearly fainted with pain and fright. Suddenly he saw a firefly, and he called out to it, "O Firefly, will you help me to get away from here?"

"Poor boy!" replied the Firefly, stopping to look at Pinocchio; "how did you ever get your legs caught in that trap?"

"I came into the field in order to get a bunch of grapes and —"

"But are the grapes yours?"

"No."

"Then who has taught you to steal other people's things?"

"I was hungry."

"Hunger, my boy, is not a good reason for stealing anybody's things."

"That is true! that is true!" cried Pinocchio, weeping; "and another time I will not do it."

Just here the conversation was interrupted by the sound of footsteps that came nearer and nearer. The owner of the field had come on tiptoe to see if one of the Weasels that ate his chickens at night had been caught. He was greatly surprised when, taking out a dark lantern, he saw, instead of a Weasel, a boy.

"Ah, you little thief!" said the angry farmer. "Then you are the one that carries away my chickens!"

"I? No," cried Pinocchio, sobbing. "I went into the field for a bunch of grapes."

"He who steals grapes is also capable of stealing chickens. Leave it to me; I will give you a lesson that you will remember for some time."

He opened the trap, took the marionette by the back of the neck like a kitten, and carried him to his house. When he reached his door he said to Pinocchio: "Now it is late and I want to go to bed. We will settle our affairs to-morrow. Meanwhile, as my dog died to-day, I will put you into his house. I will make you my watchdog."

No sooner said than done. He took a dog collar and put it on Pinocchio's neck. Attached to this collar was a chain that was fastened to the wall.

"If it begins to rain to-night," said the farmer, "there is some straw inside that has served as a bed for the dog for four years. You may go in and rest there. And if robbers come into the yard, remember to watch them carefully and to bark."

After this last warning the farmer entered his house, closing the door noisily; and the poor marionette was left squatting in the barnyard more dead than alive from cold, hunger, and fear. From time to time he placed his hands between his collar and his neck because the collar hurt him, saying to himself as he did so: "I deserve it all. I wanted to run away. I wanted to listen to the advice of bad companions, and that is the reason why I am so unhappy. If I had been a good boy as so many boys are, if I had wished to study and to work, if I had remained at home with my papa, I should not find myself here now, sleeping in a dog house and watching a chicken coop! Oh, if only I could begin all over again! But now it is too late."

Having thought all this, he entered the dog house and fell asleep.

CHAPTER XXII

After he had slept two hours he was awakened at midnight by a whispering which sounded like *pist! pist!* It appeared to come from the barnyard. He put his nose out of the hole in the dog house and saw four little beasts that looked somewhat like cats. But they were not cats; they were Weasels, — carnivorous animals who eat young chickens. One of the Weasels, leaving his companions, went to the hole in the dog house and said in a low voice, "Good evening, Bruno."

"I am not called Bruno."

"Oh, then, who are you?"

"I am Pinocchio."

"What are you doing here?"

"I am playing watchdog."

"Oh, where is Bruno? Where is the old dog that lived in this house?"

"He died this morning."

"Dead? Poor beast! He was so good! But judging from your face you are also a nice dog."

"Excuse me, I am not a dog."

"What are you?"

"I am a marionette."

"And you play watchdog?"

"Yes, it is true; I do so for a punishment."

"Well, I propose to you the same agreement that I had with the dead Bruno. Are you willing?"

"What are the conditions?"

"We will come here once a week, as we have done in the past, to pay a nocturnal visit to this chicken house; and we will carry away eight chickens. Of these we will eat seven and give you one, on condition — understand well — that you will pretend to sleep and not come out and bark and thus awaken the farmer."

"And Bruno did that?" asked Pinocchio.

"Oh, yes, and we got along very nicely. You sleep quietly and you may be sure that before we go away we will leave a nice fat chicken for your breakfast to-morrow morning. Do you understand?"

"Very well," replied Pinocchio. But he shook his head as if he would have said, "In a little while we will talk about this again."

When the four Weasels felt that they were free from harm they walked toward the chicken coop, which was very near the dog house. They opened the door with their teeth and nails and filed in one by one. But they were hardly inside when they heard the door close with a bang.

Who was it that had closed the door? Why, it was Pinocchio, who, not contented with the latch that held the door, placed a big stone there besides. And then he began to bark, and he barked just like a watchdog — *bu! bu! bu! bu!*

At that sound the farmer jumped out of bed, took his gun, and, coming to the window, said, "What is the matter?"

"The robbers are here," cried Pinocchio.

"Where are they?"

"In the chicken coop."

"I will come down right away."

Before any one could say "Boo!" the farmer came down. After he had caught the four Weasels and put them into a sack, he looked at the sack with genuine satisfaction and said: "You, then, are the ones who have been stealing my chickens! I ought to punish you, but you are beneath my notice. I will content myself instead with carrying you to the town near by, where they will take you off my hands. It is an honor you do not deserve, but generous men do not mind taking this little trouble."

Then, approaching Pinocchio, he caressed him, and among other things asked him : " How did you ever catch these four robbers ? And to think that Bruno, my good and faithful Bruno, could not do it ! "

The marionette then would have told all he knew about the shameful contract between the dog and the Weasels ; but remembering that the dog was dead, he said to himself : " Why should I accuse the dead ? The dead are dead and the best thing to do is to leave them in peace."

" Were you asleep when the Weasels came into the yard ? " asked the farmer.

" I was asleep," replied Pinocchio, "but they awoke me with their chattering, and one came to my house and said : 'If you promise not to bark and not to wake up the farmer, we will give you a nice fat chicken for a present.' You understand? How could they have the face to say that to me ? I am only a marionette and have all the faults of marionettes, but I never enter into a contract with thieves."

" Brave boy ! " cried the farmer, patting him on the shoulder. " These sentiments do you honor, and to prove to you my great satisfaction I leave you free to return to your house."

And he took off the dog's collar.

CHAPTER XXIII

As soon as Pinocchio was relieved from the weight of the hard and humiliating collar he started to run across the fields; and he did not stop one minute until he had reached the road that led to the house of the Fairy.

When he reached the road he looked down on the forest where he had unfortunately met the Fox and the Cat, and there in the middle he saw the great oak to which they had hanged him. He looked in the direction of the little white house where the Fairy with the Blue Hair lived, but he could not find it at all.

Then a feeling of sadness came over him. Nevertheless he ran as fast as his legs would take him and in a few minutes he reached the field where the little white house had stood. But the white house was there no more. There was instead

a little marble slab on which were cut the following words :

Here lies
The Fairy with the Blue Hair
Dead with Grief
For having been abandoned by her
Little Brother Pinocchio.

As he could not read he did not know what to
do.   The Talking Cricket happened to be near
and read it for him.   I leave you to imagine how
the marionette felt when he understood the mean-
ing of those words.   He fell to the ground and,
covering the marble slab with kisses, cried as if his
heart would break.   He cried all night and all the
next morning, until he had no more tears left.   His
cries and sobs were so loud that all the hills round
about repeated them.

"Oh, my little Fairy, why are you dead?" he
cried.   "Why, instead of you, am I not dead?
Oh, my dear little Fairy, tell me where I can find
my papa.   I wish to be with him and never leave
him any more.   Oh, tell me that it is not true that
you are dead.   If you truly love me, if you like
your little brother, come back! return to life!
Does it not make you unhappy to see me left all
alone by everybody?   If the assassins come and
hang me to a tree again, I shall die this time for

sure. What can I do alone in this world, now that I have lost my papa and you? Who will give me anything to eat? Where shall I sleep at night? Who will make my clothes? Oh, it would be better, a hundred times better, that I should die! Yes, I wish to die! *Ih! ih! ih!*"

While he despaired in this manner he wished to pull out his hair; but his hair being of wood he was not able to raise even a lock.

A large Dove who was flying around, seeing the little marionette leaning on the marble slab, stopped, and, hovering in the air, said, "Tell me, my little boy, what are you doing down there?"

"Do you not see that I am crying?" said Pinocchio, raising his head toward the voice and drying his eyes with the sleeve of his jacket.

"Tell me," added the Dove, "do you not know among your companions a marionette who is called Pinocchio?"

"Pinocchio? Did you say Pinocchio?" cried the marionette, jumping to his feet; "I am Pinocchio."

When the Dove heard this he flew down to the ground. He was as large as a turkey cock.

"Do you also know Geppetto?" asked the Dove.

"Do I know him? He is my poor papa. Has he asked you about me? Can you take me to him? Is he alive? Tell me, is he alive?"

"I left him three days ago on the seashore."

"What was he doing?"

"He was making a little boat in order to cross the ocean. For four months the poor man has been looking for you, and not being able to find you he began to build a boat and now he is going to look for you in another country."

"How far is it to the shore?" asked Pinocchio.

"A thousand miles."

"A thousand miles! Oh, Dove! Oh, if only I had a pair of wings!"

"If you wish to go, I will carry you."

"How?"

"On my back. Are you heavy?"

"No, indeed. I am as light as a feather."

And then without saying anything further, Pinocchio jumped on the back of the Dove and put a leg back of each wing just like a man on horseback. He then cried to the Dove, "All ready, go!" The Dove spread his wings and in a few moments they almost touched the clouds. Arriving at that extraordinary height, the marionette had the curiosity to turn around and look down. He was so scared when he took a view of the country below that he was obliged to put his arms around the Dove's neck.

They flew all day long. Toward evening the Dove said, "I am very thirsty."

"I am very hungry," added Pinocchio.

"Let us stop at this dove house a few minutes, and afterward we will start on our way again, so as to be at the shore to-morrow morning."

They entered a dove house which they found deserted except that there was a little basin of water and also a small basket of chick peas placed near the door.

In all his life the marionette had never been able to eat chick peas; to hear the name always made him sick. But that night he ate them ravenously, and when he had nearly finished he turned to the Dove and said, "I would never have believed that chick peas could taste so good."

"It is well to know, my boy," replied the Dove, "that when you are truly hungry even the chick pea seems delicious. Hunger has no whims or fancies."

Having eaten their lunch quickly, they started on their journey. The next morning they arrived on the seashore.

The Dove placed Pinocchio on the ground, and, not wishing the annoyance of hearing himself thanked for his good action, flew suddenly away and disappeared.

The shore was crowded with people who were crying and gesticulating, looking toward the sea.

"What has happened?" asked Pinocchio of an old woman.

"There is an old man, who, having lost his little boy, ventured to go to sea to-day in search of him, and the water is so rough that we are afraid he will sink."

"Where is the boat?"

"There it is; follow my finger," said the old lady, pointing to a little boat that from where they stood looked like a walnut shell with a very small man inside.

"It is my papa! It is my papa!"

Meanwhile the little boat, tossed around by the waves, now disappeared between the billows, now floated on top. Pinocchio, standing on a point of a high reef, called his papa by name and made many signals with his arms and finally with the

cap on his head. It appeared that Geppetto, although very far away from the shore, recognized him, because he also raised his cap and made it clearly understood that he would come to shore were it not that he was prevented by the heavy seas.

All of a sudden there came a terrible wave and the boat disappeared. They waited on shore to see it rise but it was never seen again.

"Poor man!" said the fishermen; but they could not help him so they turned away.

Then they heard a cry. Looking around, they saw a little boy on the top of a reef throw himself into the water.

"I want to save my papa," he said.

Pinocchio, being made of wood, floated easily, and he could swim like a fish. Now he was seen to disappear under the water, carried by the current; now he appeared again, striking out against the waves. The fishermen watched him until he was so far from shore that they could not see him any longer.

"Poor boy!" they said; and, as they could do nothing for him, they went home.

CHAPTER XXIV

Animated by the hope of arriving in time to save his father, Pinocchio swam all night. And what a horrible swim that was! It rained, hailed, thundered, and lightened so hard that the night appeared like day.

In the morning he saw a shore line. It was an island in the middle of the sea. He tried to reach that sand bank, but it was useless. The waves tossed him about like a straw. At last, by good fortune, there came a tremendous wave that hurled him right upon the shore. The force with which he struck the ground was so great that it nearly broke his bones; but he said, "I have been very lucky to escape this time."

In the meantime the weather cleared. The sun appeared in all its splendor and the sea became as smooth as oil. Then the marionette laid his clothes out on the sand and sat in the sun to dry himself. He looked all around, but he saw nothing of the little boat that contained his papa.

"I should like to know the name of this island," he said to himself. "I should like to know, at least, if it is inhabited by kind people who do not hang boys to trees; but whom can I ask if there is no one here?"

The idea of finding himself alone on an island in the sea made him very sad and he began to cry. Suddenly he saw, passing by not very far from shore, a large Fish, who went about his business quietly with his head above the water. The marionette called in a loud voice, so as to make himself heard, "Hello, Mr. Fish! Will you allow me one word?"

"Two," replied the Fish, who was so polite a dolphin that it would be hard to find his equal in the sea.

"Will you please tell me if in this island I can find something to eat without being eaten?"

"I am sure of it," replied the Dolphin. "You will find some people not far from here."

"And what street must I take?"

"Take that little road to the left and follow your nose. You cannot mistake it."

"Tell me, please, another thing. You travel so much in the sea, both by day and by night, that perhaps you have seen a little boat with my papa in it."

"And who is your papa?"

"He is the best in the world, and I am the worst son that can possibly be."

"With the terrible storm that we had last night the boat must have sunk."

"And my papa?"

"By this time he must have been swallowed by the Dogfish who for several days has been playing havoc in these waters."

"Is the Dogfish very large?" asked Pinocchio, who already trembled with fear.

"Large?" replied the Dolphin. "Why, you can get an idea of him when I tell you that he is as large as a five-story house and his mouth is so big that he can swallow, at one gulp, a train of cars with the engine attached!"

"Oh, dear me!" cried the marionette, very much scared. Turning to the Dolphin, he said hurriedly, "Good-by, Mr. Fish; excuse me, and a thousand thanks for your kindness."

Having said this, Pinocchio took the little road and ran as quickly as he could. At every slight noise he heard he looked around, for fear he might be followed by the terrible Dogfish as big as a five-story house, and with a mouth large enough to swallow a train of cars with the engine attached.

After having run for half an hour, he arrived at a little country called "The Country of the Busy Bees." The streets were filled with those who ran here and there attending to their little duties, everybody having something to do.

"I understand!" exclaimed that good-for-nothing Pinocchio. "This country is not for me. I was not born to work."

Meanwhile he was very hungry because he had eaten nothing for twenty-four hours, — not even a chick pea. What could he do? There were only two ways to get food, — either to beg or to work for it. To ask for alms he was ashamed, because his papa had told him that the only ones who had a right to beg were the truly poor, sick, or blind. The poor deserve help as do those also who are too old to work. All the others must do something, and if they suffer from hunger it is the worse for them.

Just then there passed a man, all perspiring, who was pulling two wagons filled with coal. Pinocchio, judging from his face that he was a good man, lowered his eyes for shame, and said in an under-

tone, "Will you please give me a penny? I am dying of hunger."

"Not a cent," replied the coal man; "but I will give you five if you will help me pull this wagon up the hill."

"I am surprised," replied the marionette, almost offended. "I was not made a mule; I have never pulled a wagon in all my life."

"The worse for you!" replied the coal man. "Then, my boy, if you are dying with hunger, eat a couple of slices of your pride and take care that it does not give you indigestion."

After a few moments a bricklayer passed along, carrying on his shoulder a basket of lime.

"Good gentleman, will you be kind enough to give a penny to a poor boy who is dying with hunger?"

"Come with me, and I will give you five if you will carry a basket of lime for me."

"But the lime is heavy," replied Pinocchio, "and I do not want to get tired."

"If you do not want to get tired, my boy, go hungry. Good-by."

In less than half an hour twenty other people walked by and they all said to Pinocchio: "Shame on you! Instead of finding a little work and earning some money, you stand there and beg like a vagabond."

Finally along came a good woman who carried two pitchers of water.

"Will you be so good as to give me a sip of water?" asked Pinocchio, who was burning with thirst.

"Certainly, my boy," said the good woman, placing the two pitchers on the ground.

When Pinocchio had drunk like a sponge he muttered, drying his mouth, "If I could only eat as much as I drank!"

The good woman, hearing these words, replied quickly, "If you will help me carry one of these pitchers of water up the hill, I will give you a nice piece of bread."

Pinocchio looked at the pitchers of water and did not say Yes or No.

"And with the piece of bread I will give you a piece of cauliflower dipped in oil and vinegar."

Pinocchio gave another glance at the pitcher and did not say Yes or No.

"And after the cauliflower I will give you a piece of cake."

At this Pinocchio could resist no longer. He said, "Pshaw! I will carry the pitcher to your home." The pitcher was very heavy, and not being able to carry it with his hands he put it on his head. After they arrived at the house the good woman prepared the table and gave the marionette all that she had promised. Pinocchio did not eat ; he gorged. He was so hungry that one would think he had not eaten for a week.

At length, having satisfied his hunger, he raised his head in order to thank his benefactress. Hardly had he looked at her when he uttered a long "Oh-h-h-h!"

of surprise. He remained seated as if transfixed, with his eyes opened wide, his fork in the air, and his mouth full of bread and cauliflower.

"What is the matter?" the good woman asked, laughing.

"What!" replied Pinocchio, stuttering. "What! — how you resemble — yes! yes! yes! — with the blue hair, too, just like her! Oh, my little Fairy, tell me that it is you! Do not let me cry any more! If you only knew how much I have cried! — how much I have suffered!"

And saying this, Pinocchio wept a flood of tears and, throwing himself on his knees, clung to the mysterious woman.

CHAPTER XXV

At first the good little woman pretended that she was not the Fairy with the Blue Hair ; but afterward, seeing that she was discovered and not wishing to prolong the comedy, she made herself known and said to Pinocchio: "You little rascal ! Why did you ever think that it was I ? "

"Because I like you so much. That is what told me."

"You remember me? Yet you have forgotten all I told you. And now I am old enough to be your mamma."

"And I should like very much to call you so. I should like to have a mamma like all the other boys. But how did you grow up so quickly ? "

"It is a secret."

"Teach me how to do it. I should like to grow also. Do you not see? I am always the same height."

"But you cannot grow."

"Why?"

"Because marionettes never grow. They are born marionettes, they live marionettes, and they die marionettes."

"Oh, I am tired of being always a marionette," cried Pinocchio, hitting himself on the head. "I want to become a man."

"And you will become one if you deserve to."

"Truly? And what can I do to deserve it?"

"That is easy. Accustom yourself to be a good boy."

"Oh, that is what I am now!"

"Not at all. Boys that are good are obedient, and you instead —"

"And I never obey."

"Good boys like to study and work, and you —"

"I like to play and run around."

"Good boys always tell the truth —"

"And I always tell lies."

"Good boys go to school willingly —"

"And to me school is a horrible thing. But from to-day I will change my life."

"You promise me?"

"I promise you. I want to become a good little boy and a comfort to my papa. Where is he at this time?"

"I do not know."

"Shall I ever have the good fortune to see him again?"

"I believe so. Indeed, I am sure of it."

At this reply Pinocchio was so happy that he was nearly crazy with joy. Then, raising his face and looking at the Fairy lovingly, he said to her, "Tell me, Mamma; is it true you are not dead?"

"It appears not," replied the Fairy.

"If you only knew with what grief I heard you were buried under that stone —"

"I do know it; and that is why I forgive you. The sincerity of your grief proves that you have a good heart. There is always hope for boys with good hearts. Even if they sometimes act like scamps, there is always hope that they will finally get on the right road. That is why I have come here. I will be your mamma."

"Oh, how nice!" said Pinocchio, jumping with joy.

"Will you obey me and always do what I tell you?"

"Willingly, willingly, willingly!"

"Then to-morrow," said the Fairy, "you will begin by going to school."

Pinocchio became suddenly a little less lively.

"After that you can choose a trade or some business."

Pinocchio became serious.

"What are you mumbling through your teeth?" asked the Fairy.

"I said that now it is a little late to go to school."

"No, sir. Remember that it is never too late to learn."

"But I do not wish to learn a trade."

"Why?"

"Because to work makes me tired."

"My boy, those who say that always end either in prison or in the almshouse. Every man, whether rich or poor, ought to work at something. Woe to the one that leaves himself to idleness! Idleness is a very bad disease and should be cured quickly or else when you are old you will never get over it."

These words touched the soul of Pinocchio. Quickly raising his head, he said to the Fairy: "I will study, I will work, I will do all you wish, because the life of a marionette is tiresome and I want to become a boy through and through. You have promised me that, have n't you?"

"I promise you; and now it depends upon how you behave."

CHAPTER XXVI

The next day Pinocchio went to the public school. Just imagine how the little scholars behaved when they saw a marionette in their school! They laughed out loud. Several played jokes on him. One took off his cap; another pulled his coat tails; another tried to make a mustache under his nose with ink; and another tied strings to his arms and legs in order to make him dance.

For a little while Pinocchio did not pay much attention to them, but finally, losing patience, he said: "Take care! I have not come here to be your buffoon. I respect others and I wish to be respected."

"Hurrah for the jester! He speaks like a book," shouted the little scamps, bursting forth into laughter. One of them, more impertinent than the others, stretched out his arm and tried to seize Pinocchio by the nose. But he did not have time because Pinocchio thrust his leg suddenly under the desk.

"Oh, what hard feet he has!" cried the boy, rubbing the lumps that the marionette had made.

"And what hard elbows!" said another, who for another trick had received a punch in the ribs. The fact is, that after several kicks and elbowings Pinocchio had the good will of all the boys in the school and they began to like him very much.

The school-teacher, too, praised him because he was so attentive, studious, and intelligent, — always the first to enter the school, always the last to get up when it was over. The only mistake he made was that of going with too many companions, among whom were a few who did not care to study. The teacher warned him daily, and the good Fairy, too, added her words of advice, saying, "Take care, Pinocchio! your companions will sooner or later make you lose your love for study and perhaps will bring misfortune upon you."

"There is no danger of that," replied the marionette, shrugging his shoulders and touching his forehead with his first finger as if he said, "There is much wisdom inside."

Now it happened, one beautiful day as he was going to school, that he met some of his companions who said to him, "Have you heard the news?"

"No."

"Not far from here a big dogfish as large as a mountain has floated on the beach."

"Truly? Why, it may be the same one that swallowed my papa."

"We are going to look at it. Will you come along?"

"No. I want to go to school."

"Oh, pshaw! What do you care for school? We can go there to-morrow. One lesson more or less does not matter at all."

"And what will the teacher say?"

"Oh, he will have something more to talk about to-morrow."

"And my mamma?"

"Your mamma will never know," said the wicked boys.

"Do you know what I will do?" said Pinocchio. "I want to see the dogfish very much, so I will go after school."

"Poor stupid thing!" they said. "Do you think that a dogfish of that size will wait for your slow actions? Why, he will go away, and then you will be sorry you did not go."

"How much time will it take to go there?" asked the marionette.

"In an hour we shall be back."

"Well, then, I will go. Come on! The first one there is the best," cried Pinocchio.

With that signal to start they all began to run. Pinocchio was always the first in a race; he ran as if he had wings on his feet. From time to time he turned to look at his companions, who were some distance behind. Seeing them puffing and blowing and covered with dust, he laughed out loud. The poor boy did not know what misfortune was in store for him.

CHAPTER XXVII

Arriving at the shore, Pinocchio quickly looked up and down the coast, but there was no dogfish. The sea was as still and as shiny as a looking-glass.

"Where is the dogfish?" he asked, turning to his companions.

"It has gone to breakfast," replied one of them, laughing.

"It may be that, being tired, he has gone to take a little nap," said another, laughing still louder.

From these replies Pinocchio understood that the boys had played a trick on him, making him believe a thing that was not true. He turned to them and said angrily, "And now, why did you tell me this nonsense about the dogfish?"

"Because we wanted to," they replied in a chorus.

"But why?"

"Because we wanted you to lose a day at school. Aren't you ashamed to go to school every day so steadily? And then you are too studious. Why do you do it?"

"If I study, what business is that of yours?"

"Why, it means a great deal to us because it makes us look like bad boys before the teacher."

"Why?"

"Because the scholars who study are always compared with those who do not; and we do not like it. That is all."

"And what should I do in order to make you satisfied with me?"

"You ought to hate school. Both the lessons and the teacher are boys' greatest enemies."

"And if I wish to study, what will you do?"

"We will watch for you, and at the first opportunity we will pay you up."

"You make me laugh," said the marionette, shaking his head.

"Take care, Pinocchio!" said the largest boy, going up to him and shaking his fist under his nose. "Do not make fun of us. Do not be so proud here because you have no fear of us. We have no fear of you. Remember you are alone. We are seven."

"Now, Pinocchio, I will teach you a lesson!" cried another boy. And saying that, he struck Pinocchio on the head with his fist. But it was an exchange of blows, for the lively marionette ducked

his head and replied suddenly with another blow,
and then the fight became general. Pinocchio,
although he was alone, was able to defend himself.
His hard wooden feet worked so well that they kept
all the boys at a reasonable distance. Where the
feet struck they always left a black and blue spot.

Then the boys, provoked at not being able to
get near the marionette, looked around for stones;
but there was nothing but sand. They finally took
their spelling books, geographies, histories, and
arithmetics and began hurling them at him. But
the marionette was very quick and dodged every
one, so that the books went over him and fell into
the sea.

What do you think the fishes did? Thinking
that the books might be something to eat, they
swam to the edge of the sea and looked at the
pictures; but after swallowing several pages and
frontispieces, they spat them out and made wry
faces, as if to say: "This is no food for us. We
are accustomed to eat much better stuff."

Meanwhile the combat grew fiercer until a big
old Crab came out of the water and, slowly walking up the beach, cried with the voice of a trom-
bone that has caught a cold, "Stop it! stop it!
These battles between boys always end badly.
Some misfortune is sure to happen."

Poor Crab! It was as if he had spoken to the wind. That naughty Pinocchio, turning around, said to him very rudely: "Oh, hush, ugly Crab! You would do better to eat some seaweed and cure that cold of yours. Go home to bed and take a good nap."

In the meantime the boys, who had used up all their own books, looked around and spied Pinocchio's, which they seized in less time than it takes to tell it. Among his books there was a volume bound in thick cardboard. It was a treatise on arithmetic. I will leave you to imagine how heavy it must have been. One of the boys seized the arithmetic and, taking aim, threw it at Pinocchio. Instead of hitting the marionette it struck the head of one of his companions. The boy became as white as a sheet and fell to the ground, where he lay motionless.

At the sight of the little fellow apparently dying the boys were frightened and ran away as fast as they could. In a few minutes there was no one left but Pinocchio.

Although he was more dead than alive through grief and fright, he ran to soak his handkerchief in the sea and began to bathe the temples of his poor schoolmate. Meanwhile he cried despairingly: "Eugene! My poor Eugene, open your eyes and look at me! Why do you not answer me? It was not I who hurt you. Believe me, it was not I. If you keep your eyes shut, you will make me die too. How shall I be able to go home now? What can I say to my good mamma? What will she say to me? Where shall I go? Where can I hide myself? Oh, how much better, a thousand times better, would it have been if I had gone to school! Why did I listen to them this morning? And to think that the teacher and also my mamma warned me, 'Beware of bad companions!' But I am head-strong. I am a bad, obstinate boy. I let them tell me what to do and then I do what I please. Why was I ever made? I have never had a quiet day in my life. Oh, dear! What will become of me? What will become of me?"

And Pinocchio continued to cry and weep and punch his head and call poor Eugene by name. Suddenly he heard the sound of footsteps. He turned and there were two policemen. "What are you doing there?" they asked.

"I am helping my schoolmate."

"Is he hurt?"

"It appears so."

"Worse than that," said one of them, bending down and looking at Eugene closely; "the boy is wounded in the temple. Who did it?"

"It was not I," said the marionette, who had hardly any breath left in his body.

"If you did not do it, who was it then?"

"Not I," repeated Pinocchio.

"With what was he struck?"

"With this book." And the marionette took from the ground the treatise on arithmetic, bound in thick cardboard, and handed it to the policeman.

"Whose book is this?"

"It is mine."

"That is enough. You must have done it. Stand up and come with us immediately."

"But I—"

"Come with us."

"But I am innocent."

"Come with us."

Before going away the policemen called some fishermen who at that moment were passing by in a rowboat near the shore, and said to them: "We trust this wounded boy to you. Take him to your house and help him. To-morrow we will come back and see how he is."

Then they turned to Pinocchio and, placing him between them, said: "Forward! Walk quickly! If you do not, so much the worse for you."

Without saying anything the marionette began to walk along the road that led to his home. But the poor little boy did not know whether he was in this world or not. It appeared to him that he was dreaming, and what a horrible dream it was! He was nearly crazy. His eyes saw double. His legs trembled. His tongue stuck to the roof of his mouth and he could not say a word. And yet in the midst of that species of stupidity he felt a thorn in his heart at the thought of passing under the window of the good Fairy. He would have preferred to die.

They had already reached the city and were just on the point of entering when a gust of wind blew off Pinocchio's hat and carried it along the road back of them.

"Will you allow me to get my hat?" asked Pinocchio.

"Yes, but do it quickly."

The marionette ran after it, but he did not put it on his head. He placed it between his teeth and then began to run toward the sea. He flew like a musket ball

The policemen, judging that they could not catch him, loosened a bloodhound that had gained the first premiums at all the dog shows. Pinocchio ran and the dog ran after him. All the people, hearing the noise, ran to the front doors and windows and wondered who would win the race. But the dog and Pinocchio made such a dust as they ran that they were soon hidden and were seen no more.

CHAPTER XXVIII

During that desperate run there was a terrible moment in which Pinocchio believed himself lost, for Aladdin, the dog, ran so very fast that he nearly caught him. The marionette felt behind him the warm breath of the ugly beast as he panted heavily. By good luck the beach was near and he saw the sea not far away.

As soon as he reached the water's edge the marionette gave a good spring, just like a frog, and fell into the water. Aladdin wished to stop but, carried by the impetus of his speed, he also entered the water. The unfortunate Dog did not know how to swim, so he began to gesticulate with his paws in order to right himself; but the more he gesticulated the more his head went under water. When he finally succeeded in getting his head out of water his eyes were full of tears, and, barking, he said, "I smother! I drown!"

"Die!" replied Pinocchio, who, seeing himself far away, felt that he was out of danger.

"Help me, Pinocchio! Save me from death!"

At that pitiful cry the marionette, who had really a good heart, was moved with compassion and, turning to the Dog, said to him, "But if I save you, will you promise that you will not run after me?"

"Yes, I promise you. Come quickly, for in a few minutes I shall be dead."

Pinocchio hesitated a little. Then remembering that his papa had told him that a good action is never forgotten, he swam toward Aladdin and, taking him by the tail, pulled him out and landed him safe and sound on the sand.

The poor Dog could not stand on his feet. He had unintentionally swallowed so much salt water that he was swollen like a balloon. Not wishing to trust the Dog too much, the marionette thought it prudent to throw himself again into the sea. Swimming away, he cried: "Good-by, Aladdin! Remember me to all your friends."

"Good-by, Pinocchio!" barked the Dog. "A thousand thanks for having saved my life. You have done me a great service and I shall never forget you. I hope I shall be able to repay you some day."

Pinocchio continued to swim, keeping always near the shore. Finally he thought he had arrived at a good safe place to land. Looking up and down, he saw on the reefs a sort of grotto out of which came a long thread of smoke.

" In that grotto," he said to himself, " there must be some fire. So much the better; I will go and dry myself. Then whatever will happen will happen."

Having taken this resolution he approached the reef; but when he was about to land he felt something in the water that drew him along. He tried to escape but it was too late. He found himself in a great fish net full of fishes of every kind. And then he saw coming out of the grotto a fisherman so ugly that he appeared to be a sea monster. Instead of hair he had bunches of seaweed on his head. His skin also was green; so were his eyes and his long beard. He looked like a great big lizard with arms and legs.

When the fisherman had pulled out the net he gave a great cry of satisfaction : " Thank goodness ! To-day I shall have a nice big meal."

" It is a good thing I am not a fish," said Pinocchio to himself, becoming more hopeful.

The net of fishes was carried into the grotto, which was dark and smoky. In the center was a fire, and over it a frying pan full of oil was spitting.

"Now let us see what kind of fish I have caught to-day," said the green fisherman. Putting his hand inside he drew out a number of mullets.

"These are beautiful mullets," he said, looking at them with pleasure. And after examining them he threw them into a washtub.

He repeated this operation many times, filling many tubs with other fish, his mouth watering all the time so that he could hardly wait until the fish were cooked.

"What good whitefish!"

"What exquisite bass!"

"What delicious soles!"

"What choice crabs!"

"What glorious anchovy!"

The last that remained in the net was Pinocchio. As the fisherman drew him out he looked scared and exclaimed: "What species of fish is this? I do not remember ever having seen one like it before."

He looked him all over

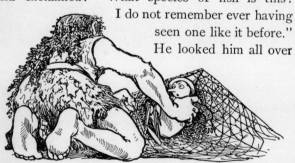

again and then said : " I understand. He belongs
to the crawfish family."

Pinocchio, mortified at being called a crawfish,
indignantly cried out : " I am not a crawfish !
Look at me ; I am a marionette."

" A marionette ! " replied the fisherman. " Well,
well ! A marionette fish is a new kind to me. All
the better ; I shall eat you with more relish."

" Eat me ? But you do not understand ! I am
not a fish. Don't you see that I reason and talk
as you do ? "

" It is true," replied the fisherman. " As I see
that you live in the water and must be a fish,
and as you know how to reason and talk, I will
respect your wisdom and will therefore let you
decide."

" What do you mean ? "

" Why, on account of my esteem and friendship
for one who knows how to reason and talk, I will
let you choose the way in which you are to be
cooked. Should you like to be boiled, or fried
in a pan with tomato sauce ? "

" To tell you the truth," replied Pinocchio, " if
I must choose, I should prefer to be set free and
to go home."

" You are joking. Do you think I would lose
the chance of eating so rare a fish ? What I will

do is to fry you with all the others. Being fried with companions is always a consolation."

At this allusion the unhappy Pinocchio began to weep. He exclaimed: "How much better would it have been if I had gone to school! I listened to the bad advice of my school friends and now I am paying for it. *Ih! ih! ih!*"

Because Pinocchio twisted and turned like an eel the fisherman took a piece of cord and bound him tightly and threw him in with the others. Then he pulled out a box of flour and, having buttered the fish all over, began to dip them into it so as to make them taste nice. The first to be put into the pan were the mullets, then the soles, then the bass, and finally it came Pinocchio's turn. The marionette, seeing himself so close to death — and such a mean death! — trembled all over with fright and had no breath left to say anything.

The poor boy looked sadly at the fisherman; but the green man, without paying any attention, buttered and floured him all over from head to foot, so that he looked like a marionette of chalk.

Then he took him by the neck and —

CHAPTER XXIX

Just as the fisherman was on the point of putting
Pinocchio into the frying pan a big Dog entered
the grotto, having been attracted by the savory
odor of the fried fish. "Go away!" cried the
fisherman, waving in his hand the marionette all
covered with flour. But the poor Dog had a hunger that demanded to be appeased. So, whining
and wagging his tail, he appeared to say, "Give me
a mouthful of fish and I will leave."

"Go away!" repeated the fisherman, raising his foot to kick him. Then the Dog, who was truly hungry, showed his terrible teeth.

At that instant there was heard in the grotto a small voice crying, "Save me, Aladdin! If you do not, I shall be fried."

The Dog recognized the voice of Pinocchio and was surprised to find that it came from the white bundle that the fisherman held in his hand. Then what did he do? He jumped up high, caught that white bundle and, holding it lightly between his teeth, ran out of the grotto like a shot.

The fisherman was greatly enraged and tried to catch him, but it was wasted time and he had to content himself with the fish that were left.

In the meantime Aladdin, finding the road that led back to the town, stopped and carefully placed Pinocchio on the ground.

"How can I thank you?" said the marionette.

"It is not necessary," said the Dog. "You have saved me and now I save you. In this world all ought to help one another."

"But how did you find the grotto?"

"After you left me I was lying on the shore when the wind carried to me the odor of fried fish. That odor gave me an appetite and I went to the place from which it came. If I had been a minute later—"

"Don't speak about it!" cried Pinocchio, trembling with fear. "Don't speak about it! If you had arrived a minute later, I should have been fried, eaten, and digested. *Brrr!* It makes me shake only to think of it!"

Aladdin, laughing, held out his paw, which Pinocchio took. After shaking hands like two good friends, they separated. The Dog went home and Pinocchio went to a little town not far away. There he asked an old man who was sitting in the doorway basking in the sun, "Tell me, do you know anything about a little boy who was wounded and who is called Eugene?"

"The boy has been carried into this town by some fishermen and he is now —"

"Not dead?" interrupted Pinocchio in great grief.

"No; he is alive and has gone home."

"Truly? truly?" cried the marionette, jumping up and down with great joy. "Then the wound was not serious?"

"No; but it might have been, for he was struck by a large book."

"And who threw it?"

"One of his companions; a certain Pinocchio."

"Who is this Pinocchio?"

"They say that he is a bad boy, a vagabond and a true scoundrel."

"That is not true."

"Do you know him then?"

"By sight," replied the marionette.

"What do you think of him?"

"He appears to me to be a good boy, a boy that wants to go to school, to study, and to obey his parents."

When the marionette had told that story he touched his nose and found that it had grown much larger. Frightened by this, he cried: "Do not believe, good man, all that I have said! I know this Pinocchio very well and I assure you that he is a bad boy, a vagabond and a scoundrel; and instead of going to school he goes with bad companions." He had hardly said these words when his nose returned to its natural size.

"And why are you covered with white?" said the old man.

"I will tell you, if you choose, but it is a long story," replied the marionette, who was ashamed to tell the reason.

"Well, my boy, you cannot go about like that. I have only a little sack that will fit you, but I will give you that with pleasure."

Without being urged further Pinocchio took the little sack and, cutting a hole in the bottom and two holes on the side with a pair of scissors, put

it over his head like a shirt. Clothed thus lightly
he took the road to his home and said to himself as he walked along: "How shall I present
myself to my good Fairy? What will she say
when she sees me? Will she pardon me the second time? Oh, no; she will not pardon me, I am
sure, because I have been a scamp and have not
kept my promise."

When he arrived at the town it was quite dark;
and because it rained very hard, he went directly
to the house of the Fairy and decided to knock at
the door. But when he reached the house his
courage failed, so instead of knocking he walked
beyond. He returned a second time to the door,
but did not knock; then he approached it another
time, but did nothing. The fourth time he trembled as he took hold of the knocker and let it fall
without much noise.

He waited and waited. In about half an hour a
window opened on the top floor (for there were four
stories to the house) and Pinocchio saw a large Snail
look out. The Snail called, "Who is it at this
hour?"

"Is the Fairy at home?" asked the marionette.

"The Fairy is sleeping and does not wish to be
awakened; but who are you?"

"It is I."

"Who is I?"

"Pinocchio."

"Who is Pinocchio?"

"The marionette who lives here with the Fairy."

"Ah, I understand," said the Snail.   "Wait there and I will come down immediately."

"Hurry, please, for I am dying of cold."

"My boy, I am a snail; and snails never hurry."

In the meantime an hour passed by, then two; and the door was not opened. Pinocchio, trembling with the cold, knocked again. At the second knock the window on the third story opened and the Snail looked out.

"Beautiful Snail," cried Pinocchio from the street, "I have waited two hours; and two hours in this weather seem like two years. Please hurry, won't you?"

"My boy," replied the Snail, "I am a snail; and snails never hurry."

Some time afterward it struck midnight; then one; then two; but the door remained always closed. Then Pinocchio, losing patience, took hold of the knocker and was about to strike with all his might when the knocker became an eel and, slipping through his hands, dropped into a stream of water that ran in the street.

"Ho! ho!" cried Pinocchio, more enraged than ever. "If the knocker disappears I will use my foot." He then kicked the door so hard that his foot went through the wood and stuck there. He tried to pull it out but he could not. Just imagine how he felt! He was obliged to wait with one foot on the ground and the other in the door until morning came.

In the morning the door was opened. The good Snail had taken nine hours in descending the stairs, and, as might have been expected, was covered with perspiration.

"What are you doing with your foot in the door?" he asked, laughing.

"I have been unfortunate. Just look, kind Snail, and help me."

"My boy, you need a carpenter, and I have never learned that trade."

"Ask the Fairy to help me."

"The Fairy is asleep and does not wish to be awakened."

"But what can I do all day with my foot fastened to the door?"

"You can amuse yourself by counting the ants that pass by."

"Bring me something to eat, won't you? I am very hungry."

"Immediately," said the Snail.

After three hours Pinocchio saw him coming with a silver vase on his head. The vase contained some bread, a piece of chicken, and four ripe apricots.

"Here is your breakfast sent to you by the Fairy."

At the sight of such food Pinocchio felt consoled. But he was deceived; for when he took the bread he found that it was chalk, that the chicken was made of cardboard, and that the four apricots were of glass.

He wanted to cry, he wanted to scream, he wanted to throw the silver vase into the house; but he was so weak that he fell down and fainted. When he came to he found himself on a sofa and the Fairy was near him.

"I will pardon you this time; but woe to you if you ever do it again!" said the Fairy.

Pinocchio promised that in future he would be good. He kept his promise the rest of the year. In fact, at the examinations he took the first honors, and the Fairy was so happy that she said to him, "To-morrow you shall have your wish."

"And that is?"

"To-morrow you shall stop being a marionette and become a real boy."

One who never saw Pinocchio cannot imagine how happy he was at this announcement. All his friends and schoolmates were invited to a great collation. The Fairy had prepared two hundred cups and saucers and four hundred little sandwiches buttered inside and out. That day promised to be a great event but —

Unfortunately in the life of a marionette there is always a *but* that spoils everything.

CHAPTER XXX

Pinocchio suddenly asked the Fairy's permission to go and invite his friends. The Fairy said: "Go and invite them, but remember to come back before night. Do you understand?"

"I promise to be back in an hour," he replied.

"Take care, Pinocchio! Boys make promises easily, but sometimes they do not keep them."

"I am not like other boys. And I shall certainly keep this promise."

"We shall see. In case you disobey it will be the worse for you."

"Why?"

"Because boys who do not pay attention to the advice of their parents always meet with misfortune."

"I have had experience," said Pinocchio; "now you will see that I obey."

"We shall see if you speak the truth."

In a little more than an hour all his friends were invited. Some accepted at once; others hesitated until they heard of the good things to eat. Then they said, "We will surely come."

Now you must know that among his companions there was one that he liked best of all. His name was Romeo; but he was nicknamed Lamp Wick, because he was as dry as a new lamp wick that people use to light their houses.

Lamp Wick was the most careless and mischievous boy in all the school, but Pinocchio liked him very much. He went to look for him so as to give him an invitation to the party next day; but he sought in vain. Where could he be? He looked here and there and finally found him under a shed of a country house.

"What are you doing here?" asked Pinocchio.

"I am waiting until it is midnight, so that I can go away."

"Where are you going?"

"Far away, far away, far away."

"I have looked for you everywhere."

"What do you want with me?"

"Have you not heard?"

"What is it?"

"To-morrow I shall no longer be a marionette; I shall become a boy like all the rest."

"Good luck to you!"

"But I want you to be there."

"I have told you that I am going away to-night."

"At what time?"

"Shortly."

"Where do you go?"

"I am going to live in a new country that is the most beautiful place in all the world. It is a true land of plenty."

"What do they call it?"

"They call it 'The Country of Playthings.' Why won't you come?"

"I? No, indeed."

"You are wrong, Pinocchio. Believe me, if you do not go away, you will be sorry. Where can you find a better place for boys? There are no schools; there are no teachers; there are no books. In that pleasant country they never study. On Saturdays you do not go to school here, and there every day is a Saturday except one, which is Sunday. Just think, the vacation begins the first day of January and ends the last day of December! That is the country for me. That is what I think all countries should be like."

"But how do you pass the days in the Country of Playthings?"

"Why, you play from morning till night. At night you go to bed, and the next morning it is the same thing all over again. How should you like it?"

"Uhm!" said Pinocchio, and he shook his head lightly as if to say, "It is a country that would please me very much."

"Then will you go with me? Yes or no."

"No, no, no! I have promised my kind Fairy to become a good boy and I wish to keep my word. The sun is going down and I must hurry. Good-by and a pleasant journey."

"Don't go away so soon. Why do you hurry?"

"Because I told the good Fairy that I would be at home before dark."

"Wait two minutes."

"No; it will be too late."

"Only two minutes."

"The Fairy will scold me."

"Let her scold. When she has scolded enough she will stop," said the little scoundrel Lamp Wick.

"And what are you going to do? Do you go alone or with company?"

"Alone? Why, there will be a hundred boys."

"Do you go on foot?"

"Oh, no! A little carriage will come soon and take me."

"How much I would give to see the carriage pass by now!"

"Why?"

"I should like to see you all start."

"If you will stay here a little while you will see them."

"No, no! I wish to go home."

"Oh, wait another two minutes."

"No; I have waited too long now. The Fairy will worry about me."

"Poor Fairy! Does she think that you will be eaten by bats?"

"But tell me," urged Pinocchio, "you are sure that in that country there is no school?"

"Not even the shadow of one."

"And no teachers?"

"Not one."

"And you are never obliged to study?"

"Never, never, never!"

"What a beautiful country!" said Pinocchio, his mouth beginning to water. "I have never been there, but I can imagine all about it."

"Why don't you come along?"

"It is useless to tempt me. I have promised to be a good boy and I wish to keep my word."

" Well, then, good-by ; remember me to all the scholars."

" Good-by, Lamp Wick. I wish you a good trip and I hope you will meet some nice new friends."

Having said this, the marionette took two steps toward home ; then he stopped and asked, " But are you sure that there are six Saturdays in the week and only one Sunday ? "

" I am positive."

" And can you say for certain that the vacation begins on the first of January and ends the last day of December ? "

" I am positive."

" What a beautiful country ! " said Pinocchio. Presently he made another start and said, " Then good-by truly this time, and I wish you a safe journey."

" Good-by."

" How soon do you start ? "

" Shortly now."

" Too bad ! I think I will wait and see you go."

" And the Fairy ? "

" It is late now, and an hour later will not make much difference."

" Poor Pinocchio ! and if the Fairy should scold ? "

" Well, let her scold. When she has scolded enough she will stop."

In the meantime it became quite dark. Suddenly as they talked they saw moving along the road a little light and heard the tooting of little trumpets so small and fine that they sounded like the buzzing of a mosquito.

"Here they are!" said Lamp Wick, standing up.

"Who is it?" asked Pinocchio, in a low voice.

"It is the carriage that is coming for me. Now will you go? Yes or no."

"But are you sure," asked the marionette, "that in that country the boys are not obliged to study?"

"Never, never, never!"

"What a beautiful country it must be!"

CHAPTER XXXI

Finally the carriage arrived without making the least noise, because the wheels were bound with tow and rags. Twelve little donkeys pulled it; they were of the same size but of different colors. Some were brown, others speckled like pepper and salt, and others were striped with bands of yellow and blue. But the most singular thing about them was this: these twelve pair of donkeys, that is, the twenty-four donkeys, instead of having shoes made of iron, had on their feet white kid boots shaped like a man's.

And the driver? Just imagine a man very fat and round, like a big ball of butter, with an oily smile, a face like an apple, and a thin, caressing voice like that of a cat trying to win the affection of its mistress!

As soon as they saw him the boys were tempted to jump into the carriage and start away for the place unknown on the geographical maps,—the Country of Playthings.

The carriage was filled with boys between eight and ten years of age, packed like sardines in a box. They were so closely huddled together that they could hardly breathe. But no one said "Oh!" No one complained. The consolation of knowing that in a few hours they would arrive in a country where there were no books, or schools, or teachers made them happy and resigned, so that they did not feel hurt, or uncomfortable, or hungry, or thirsty.

As soon as the carriage stopped, the fat driver turned to Lamp Wick and with a thousand airs and grimaces said to him, smiling, "Tell me, my pretty lad, do you wish to come with us to the most fortunate country?"

"Indeed I do."

"But I warn you that there is no place inside. As you see, it is full."

"Oh, well," replied Lamp Wick, "if there is no place inside, I will sit on top of the carriage," and he jumped up and sat beside the driver.

"And what about your friend?" said the driver, turning most politely toward Pinocchio. "What will he do? Are you coming with us also?"

"I remain here," replied Pinocchio. "I wish to return home. I prefer to study and to be a good boy."

"What good will that do you?"

"Listen to me, Pinocchio," said Lamp Wick; "come with us and always be happy."

"No, no, no!"

"Come with us and always be happy," said four others.

"Come with us and always be happy," said all the rest.

"And if I go with you, what will the good Fairy say?" asked Pinocchio, who began to feel as if he were being pulled by his sleeve.

"Do not think of that. Think of the country we shall be in. We shall be our own masters and make a fine noise all day long."

Pinocchio did not reply, but gave a sigh; then he gave another sigh; then a third sigh; finally he said: "Give me a place. I will go with you."

"All the places are full," replied the driver; "but if you wish, take my place."

"What will you do?"

"I will walk."

"No; I cannot allow that. I prefer to ride on one of the donkeys," said Pinocchio.

No sooner said than done. He approached the nearest donkey and tried to mount it; but the donkey suddenly raised his hind feet and threw Pinocchio off. Just imagine the impertinent laughter of all those boys who saw it!

Pinocchio, who was very angry, made another jump on the donkey's back. The jump was such a beautiful one that the boys began to laugh and shout, "Long live Pinocchio!" and clap their hands for joy.

When they were ready to start the donkey again raised his hind feet and gave such a strong kick that the marionette was thrown on top of a heap of gravel. The boys again laughed out loud; but the driver, instead of laughing, went to the donkey and seemed to whisper something in his left ear. Then he said to the marionette: "Remount and have no fear. That donkey had a whim in his head, but I have spoken to him and he will be more reasonable."

Pinocchio mounted and the carriage started. While the donkeys galloped along the marionette fancied that he heard a strange voice saying: "Poor simpleton! You wish to do as you please. You will be sorry."

The frightened Pinocchio looked first on one side of the road and then on the other to see whence these words came ; but he saw no one. The donkeys galloped, the carriage rolled along, the boys inside slept, Lamp Wick snored like a dormouse, and the driver sang between his teeth :

> All the night they sleep,
> And I never . . .

They made another mile. Again Pinocchio heard the voice. This time it said : " Bear in mind, simpleton, that boys who stop studying and throw away their books and do nothing but play and amuse themselves will always come to a bad end. I know it, for I have tried it, but I cannot say any more. You will cry some day as I do now, but then it will be too late."

At these whispered words the marionette was more frightened than ever. He jumped down to the ground and put his ear to the donkey's nose. Imagine how surprised he was when he perceived that the donkey wept just like a little boy ! " Mr. Driver," cried Pinocchio, " do you know that this donkey can cry ? "

" Let him cry. He will laugh when he has some hay."

" But who taught him to speak ? "

"He learned to say a few words in a country where he lived for a little while."

"Poor beast!"

"Do not waste your time pitying a donkey when he cries. Jump on his back and let us go. The night is fresh and the road is long."

Pinocchio obeyed in silence. The carriage moved on, and when the sun came up they arrived at the Country of Playthings.

This country did not resemble any other in the world. The population was composed entirely of boys. The oldest was thirteen years and the youngest not under eight. In the streets there was a noise, a running around, and a blowing of trumpets that would make your head ache. Everywhere groups of boys played at marbles, at shinny, at ball; some rode on velocipedes and wooden horses; some played hide and seek; others played tag; some sang; others jumped over benches; some walked on their hands with their feet in the air; others tried to kick over their heads; some laughed; some called; some whistled; some made a noise like a hen that has just laid an egg. In fact, there was such a pandemonium that you would have had to put cotton in your ears.

As soon as Pinocchio, Lamp Wick, and all the other newcomers in this country had arrived, they ran around with the others and began to play. Who could have been happier or more contented than they? "Oh, what a beautiful life this is!" said Pinocchio, running after Lamp Wick.

"See; was I not right?" said the latter. "You did not wish to come. To think that you should want to return to the Fairy's house and study! If to-day you are free from all the annoyances of school and its troubles, you should thank me. True friends are the only ones who know how to render favors to one another."

"It is true, Lamp Wick. If to-day I am a free and happy boy, I owe it all to you. Yet the teacher used to say to me, 'Do not go with Lamp Wick because he is a bad companion.'"

"Poor Teacher!" replied the other, shaking his head.

So they played in the country for five months. They never saw a book; never studied a minute. They played from morning till night. One morning when Pinocchio awoke he was surprised to find what had happened, and it made him very unhappy.

CHAPTER XXXII

What was the surprise? I will tell you, my dear little reader. The surprise was that when Pinocchio awoke one morning and happened to scratch his head, he perceived — just imagine what he perceived! You know that when the marionette was born he had very little ears, so little that you could scarcely see them. Fancy, then, how surprised he was, when he put his hand to his head, to find that his ears had grown long! He went quickly in search of a mirror, but not finding any he emptied some water into a basin. Then, looking at his reflection, he saw something that he certainly did not expect to see, — two beautiful, long, donkey ears.

I will leave you to imagine the grief, the shame, the desperation of Pinocchio. He cried and screamed and beat his head against the wall; but his ears grew and grew and grew until hair began to show on the tops.

At the sound of his heartrending cries a Dormouse, who lived on the first floor, entered the room. Seeing the marionette in great anguish, he asked eagerly, "What is the matter, my dear little lodger?"

"I am sick, Dormouse; very sick, and with a sickness that alarms me. Do you understand the pulse?"

"A little."

"See, then, if I have a fever."

The Dormouse took Pinocchio's wrist in his paw and, after having tested his pulse, said, "My friend, it grieves me to tell you bad news."

"What is it?"

"You have a bad fever."

"What kind?"

"The donkey fever."

"I do not understand that disease," replied Pinocchio, who really understood very well.

"I will explain it to you. Know, then, that in two or three hours you will be a donkey, a real donkey, like those that pulled the carriage which brought you here."

"Oh, what shall I do? what shall I do?" cried

Pinocchio, pulling his ears so hard that it must have hurt him.

"My dear," said the Dormouse, "what are you trying to do? You must know that it is a written decree that those boys who do not wish to study, who hate books and teachers, and who spend the whole day enjoying themselves, end by becoming little donkeys."

"Is that really true?" asked the marionette.

"Of course it is. And now it is of no use to cry. You should always think first."

"But the fault is not mine. The fault, believe me, is all Lamp Wick's."

"Who is Lamp Wick?"

"A friend of mine. I wished to go back to school and be an honor to the good Fairy; but

Lamp Wick said to me, 'In the Country of Playthings no one studies, and we can play from morning till night.'"

"Why did you follow the advice of a bad friend?"

"Why? Because, Dormouse, I am a foolish, heartless marionette. Oh, if I had had a little bit of heart, I should never have left my good Fairy, who loved me like a mamma and did much for me. And by this time I should have been a little boy like all the rest instead of a marionette. Oh, if I had not met Lamp Wick!"

And he walked toward the door. But when he had gone outside he remembered his donkey ears; and, being ashamed of himself, what do you think he invented? He made a dunce cap and, putting it on his head, pulled it down over his ears. Then he went out and looked for Lamp Wick. He looked in the streets, in the square, in the theater, in fact, everywhere; but he could not find him. He asked if any one had seen him, but no one knew where he was. He then went to his house and knocked at the door.

"Who is there?" asked Lamp Wick from the inside.

"It is I," replied Pinocchio.

"Wait a little and I will open the door."

After half an hour the door opened and Pinocchio saw his friend, also in a dunce cap which covered his ears.

At the sight of that cap Pinocchio felt somewhat consoled, and he thought to himself, "He has the same trouble and also suffers from donkey fever."

Feigning not to see anything, he asked gayly, "How are you, my dear Lamp Wick?"

"Like a rat in a cake of cheese."

"Are you telling me the truth?"

"Why should I tell a story?"

"Excuse me; but why do you wear that cap then?"

"A doctor ordered it because my knees hurt. And you, Pinocchio, why do you wear one?"

"The doctor ordered it because I had corns on my feet."

"Oh, poor Pinocchio!"

"Oh, poor Lamp Wick!"

After these words there was a long silence during which time the two friends looked at each other. Finally the marionette said in a kind voice, "Raise your cap just a little, will you?"

"Never! And you?"

"Never! You see I have an ear that is very painful."

"So have I."

"You, too? And which ear hurts?"

"Both. And you?"

"Both. Can it be the same malady?"

"I fear so."

"Do you wish to please me, Lamp Wick?"

"With all my heart."

"Let me see your ears."

"Oh, no! First let me see yours."

"No; you ought to do it first."

"No; after you always."

"Then," said the marionette, "let us make a contract."

"All right."

"Let us take off our caps together."

"All right."

"Look out then." And Pinocchio began to count: "One, two, three!"

At the word "three," the boys took off their caps and threw them into the air. And then they laughed and laughed and laughed until they were compelled to hold their sides. Suddenly Lamp Wick stopped and, changing color, said to his friend, "Help! oh, help me, Pinocchio!"

"What is the matter?"

"Oh, dear me! I cannot stand up any longer."

"I cannot, either," cried Pinocchio.

Even while they were speaking they fell on their hands and began to run around the room on all fours. And while they ran their arms became legs, their faces changed, and their bodies were covered with long hair. But the moment that was most horrible for each unfortunate was when he felt a tail swishing behind him. Overcome by shame and grief, they tried to talk. But they could not do it. Instead of sobs and lamentations there came the bray of a donkey and it sounded like "Y-a, y-a."

In the meantime there was a knock on the door and they heard a voice outside saying: "Open the door! I am the driver of the carriage that brought you here. Open quickly, or woe be unto you!"

CHAPTER XXXIII

Seeing that the door did not open, the driver gave it a violent kick. It fell and he entered the room saying in his usual oily way, "Good boys! You bray very well. I recognize your voices and here I am to take you away."

At these words the two little donkeys became quiet. They lowered their heads and ears and put their tails between their legs.

At first the driver patted them and smoothed their hair. After that he pulled out some leather straps and bridled them both. When he had curried them so that they looked like two looking-glasses, he took them to the square in the hope of selling them and making a good trade.

The purchasers soon made their appearance. Lamp Wick was bought by a farmer whose donkey had died the day before from overwork. Pinocchio was bought by the director of a company of clowns and circus men, so that he could be taught to do tricks and capers.

And now, my little readers, do you understand what the trade of the driver was? That monster, who had a face of milk and honey, went from time to time through the world with a carriage and collected, by promises, all the naughty boys that were tired of books and school. After he had filled his carriage he took them to the Country of Playthings, where they passed all the time in playing and having fun. When these poor deluded boys had played for a certain time they turned into donkeys, which he led away and sold in the town. By this means he had become very rich, — in fact a millionaire.

What happened finally to Lamp Wick I do not know. I know, however, that Pinocchio led a very hard and weary life. When he was taken to a stall his new master emptied some straw into the manger; but Pinocchio, after he had eaten a mouthful, spat it out. Then the master, scolding, gave him some hay; but that did not please him.

"Ah! You do not like hay?" cried the master, in anger. "I will teach you better manners."

He then took a whip and gave the donkey a crack on the legs. Pinocchio, in great pain, gave a long bray, as if to say, "Y-a, y-a, I cannot digest straw."

"Then eat hay," replied the master, who understood the donkey dialect very well.

"Y-a, y-a. Hay gives me a headache."

"You mean that a donkey like you wants to eat chicken and capon?" added the master; and he gave him another lash with the whip.

At the second rebuke Pinocchio, for prudence' sake, kept quiet and said nothing. Meanwhile the stall was closed and Pinocchio remained alone; and because he had not eaten anything for hours he grew very hungry. He opened his mouth and was surprised to find that it was so large.

He finally looked around, and not finding anything in the manger but hay, took a little. After having chewed it well he winked his eye and said: "This hay is not bad at all. But how much better off I should have been if I had not run away! Now I should be eating something nice instead of this dry stuff. Oh me! oh me! oh me!"

When he awoke the next morning he looked into his manger, but he had eaten all the hay. Then he took a mouthful of straw and tried that. It did not taste so good as rice *alla Milanese* or macaroni *alla Napolitana;* but he managed to eat it.

"Oh me!" he said while he ate; "oh, if I could only warn other boys of my misfortune, how happy I should be! Oh me! oh me!"

"Oh me!" repeated the master, entering the stall at that moment. "Do you think, donkey, that I have bought you just to watch you eat and drink? Oh no! I bought you so that you could earn some money for me. Come with me and I will teach you how to jump and bow; and then you must dance the waltz and the polka and stand up on your hind legs."

Poor Pinocchio! He had a hard struggle. It took him three months to learn these things and he received many a blow from his teacher.

The day finally came when the master could announce to the public a most extraordinary spectacle. Posters of all colors were pasted everywhere and they read thus:

GRAND ENTERTAINMENT
WILL TAKE PLACE TO-NIGHT

There will be the usual wonderful jumps and most surprising exercises

Executed by all the Artists

And by all the horses in this remarkable Company

AND MORE ! !

There will be presented for the first time The Famous Donkey

PINOCCHIO
Called
THE DANCING STAR

The Theater will be as bright as day

That night, as you can easily imagine, there was not a seat to be had in the house, and all the standing room was taken an hour before the show began. The whole theater swarmed with little children and babies of all ages, who were wild to see the famous donkey Pinocchio dance.

When the first part of the performance was over the master, in an evening coat, with white trousers and little black boots, presented himself to the public and, after making a profound bow, shouted:

Respected public, ladies and gentlemen, — The humble manager of this performance, passing through this great metropolis, has told me to say that it is his wish to present to this intelligent and honorable audience a celebrated donkey that has already had the honor of dancing before His Majesty the Emperor at all the principal courts of Europe.

This discourse was received with much laughter and applause; but the applause redoubled and became a species of hurricane at the sight of the donkey Pinocchio on the stage. He was dressed up beautifully. He had a new bridle of shining leather with buckles of polished brass; two white camellias tied to his ears; his mane divided in many curls tied with red silk; a large band of gold and silver tied around his waist; and his tail interlaced with beautiful ribbons of all colors. In fact, he was the most gorgeous donkey that ever was seen.

The master then presented him to the public with these words:

My respected auditors, — I will not take up much of your time, but I wish to tell you of the great difficulties I encountered in taming and teaching this animal. Observe, I pray you, how savagely violent are his eyes. It seemed almost impossible that I should be able to train him to behave like other domestic animals. All my gentleness was received with scorn and I was obliged to talk to him in the dialect of the whip. However, I noticed on his head this little lump. It is hard to see, but it can be felt very easily. According to the medical faculty of Paris this would indicate a passion for dancing, and I therefore began to teach him the art of using his feet. And now you may judge for yourselves whether or not I have succeeded.

Here the master made another profound bow and, turning to Pinocchio, said, "Before going through your exercises salute this respected and intelligent audience."

Pinocchio, obeying, fell on his knees and stayed there until the master cracked his whip and cried, "Now walk." Then the donkey stood up on his four feet and began to walk around in a circle.

"Now trot." And Pinocchio began to trot.

"Gallop." And Pinocchio began to gallop.

"Now full speed." And Pinocchio ran as hard as he could. While he was running the master, raising a pistol, fired twice.

At that sound the donkey, pretending to be hit, fell flat on the floor as if he were dead.

Raising himself in the midst of a shower of applause which could be heard for miles, Pinocchio looked at the audience. As he looked he saw a beautiful lady wearing around her neck a large gold chain from which hung a medallion. On the medallion was engraved the picture of a marionette.

"That is my picture! That lady is the Fairy!" said Pinocchio to himself, recognizing her instantly. He tried to cry, "Oh, my Fairy! oh, my Fairy!" But instead of these words there came from his throat such a braying that everybody laughed, especially the boys.

Then the master, in order to teach him better manners than to bray at the audience, gave him a blow on the nose with the handle of the whip. The poor donkey licked his nose at least a dozen times because it pained him so. But what was his desperation when, turning around a second time and looking toward the Fairy, he found that she had disappeared.

He thought he should die. His eyes filled with tears and he began to cry. No one, however, saw it, not even the master, who, cracking his whip, cried, "Now show the people how well you can dance."

Pinocchio tried two or three times; but every time he came before the audience his feet slipped from under him. Finally, in a great effort, his hind foot slipped so badly that he fell to the floor in a heap. When he got up he was so lame that he could hardly walk and had to be taken to his stall.

"Bring out Pinocchio! We want the donkey! Bring him out!" cried the boys in the theater,

who had seen the pitiful sight. But the donkey could not be seen any more that night. The next morning the veterinary, that is, the doctor of beasts, when he saw the poor donkey, declared that he would be lame all through life. Then the master said to the stable boy: "What can we do with a lame donkey? To keep him would be feeding one more mouth for nothing. Take him to the square and sell him."

When they arrived at the square they immediately found a buyer who asked the price.

"Four dollars," replied the stable boy.

"I will give you twenty-five cents for him. Do not think that I buy him for hauling. Oh, no; I want him to skin. I see that his skin is very hard, — just the thing for a drum or a tambourine."

Just imagine how Pinocchio felt when he heard that he was worth only twenty-five cents! Then, too, to be used as a drum to be beaten upon all the time!

The buyer had hardly paid for him when he led him to the top of a cliff on the shore of the sea, and, tying a heavy stone around his neck and binding his feet together with cords, threw him over the edge.

The donkey, with this heavy weight around his neck, sank to the bottom immediately. The buyer,

who had one end of the rope in his hands, sat down
and waited awhile, so that the donkey would have
time to drown.

CHAPTER XXXIV

When the donkey had been under water about
an hour, the buyer, talking to himself, said : " Now
my nice-looking lame donkey ought to be dead by
this time. I will pull him up and then set to work
to make a drum." And he began to pull the rope
with which he had bound the donkey. He pulled
and pulled and pulled, until he saw coming out of
the water — what do you think ? Instead of a
dead donkey he saw a marionette, alive and kicking, struggling and twisting like an eel.

Seeing the wooden marionette, the buyer thought
that he was dreaming ; and he stood there astonished,

with his mouth open-and his eyes nearly out of his head. When he found words he said, "Where is the little donkey that I threw overboard?"

"I am that little donkey," replied the marionette, laughing.

"You?"

"I."

"Ah! You cheat! Do you think that you can make fun of me?"

"Make fun of you? On the contrary, I speak to you seriously."

"But how is it that a little while ago you were a donkey and now, after you have been in the water for an hour, you are a wooden marionette?"

"It is the effect of the sea water. The sea never tells its secrets, and this is one of its little tricks."

"Take care, marionette, take care! Do not think that you can pull wool over my eyes. Woe to you if I lose my patience!"

"Very well. Do you wish to know the true story? Untie my legs and I will tell you."

The buyer, curious to know the true story, untied the knots that bound the marionette; and then Pinocchio, finding himself as free as a bird in the air, said: "Know, then, that I was at first a wooden marionette as I am to-day. But I was on the point of becoming a boy, just like other boys, when I listened to the advice of a bad companion, and one morning I awoke and found myself turned into a donkey with big ears and a beautiful tail. What shame I felt when I saw that I had a tail! I was then led to a square where a master bought me and taught me to do tricks and dance. One night, when I was performing, I fell and sprained my leg so badly that I could hardly stand on it. Then the master, who did not know what to do with a lame donkey, sold me to you."

"Yes; I paid twenty-five cents for you. But who will give me my money back?"

"Yes; you bought me and planned to beat me by placing my skin over a drum."

"Where shall I find another skin?"

"That is not for me to say."

"Tell me, then, if you please, is your story finished?"

"No," replied the marionette; "there are a few more words, and then I shall be through. After you bought me you led me here to kill me; but then, being a humane man, you decided to drown me. This delicate attention on your part is most honorable and I shall always remember your goodness. You would have succeeded if it had not been for the good Fairy."

" Who is the Fairy ? "

" She is my mamma, who is like all other mammas in this world. She liked me and tried to make me a good and studious boy. As soon as the good Fairy saw me in danger of drowning she sent a school of fishes, which, believing that I was really dead, began to eat me. And what mouthfuls they took ! Some ate my ears ; some my neck and mane ; some the skin on my legs ; some the hair on my back ; and among them there was one big fish that ate my tail at one bite. When the fish had eaten everything they finally came to the bones, — or rather, they came to the wood. Finding that too hard for their teeth, they went away and did not even look back to say good-by."

" I do not believe your silly story," said the buyer, now very angry. " I know I have spent twenty-five cents and I want my money again. Do you know what I will do ? I will carry you back to the square and sell you for a piece of kindling wood."

" All right ! " said Pinocchio. Thus saying, he jumped into the water and, swimming lightly, drew away from the coast, calling to the poor buyer : " Good-by, dear sir ! If you want a drumhead, don't forget me." And then he laughed and kept on swimming.

After a little time he turned around and shouted : "Good-by, dear sir ! If you want a piece of kindling wood, don't forget me."

Almost in the twinkling of an eye he was so far away that he could hardly be seen ; that is, one could see only a little black point on the water, splashing around just like a jolly dolphin.

Meanwhile, as Pinocchio swam around, he saw not very far away a rock which looked like white marble. On the top of the rock there was a beautiful Goat that bleated and made a sign to him to come nearer. The most singular thing about this goat was the color of its wool. It was not white or black or any color that other goats have. It was blue, just like the hair of the beautiful Fairy.

I will leave you to imagine how the heart of Pinocchio began to beat. He redoubled his efforts to reach the rock. Already he was halfway there when he saw coming out of the water the horrible head of a sea monster, with mouth opened wide like an abyss and three rows of teeth that would frighten you, even to see them painted in a picture book.

Can you guess who that monster was ? It was no other than the huge Dogfish described several times in this story. On account of his destructive and bloodthirsty nature he was called "The Attila of fishes and fishermen."

Imagine the fright of poor Pinocchio at the sight of the monster! He sought to avoid him, — to change his road. He tried to escape; but that immense open mouth came always toward him with the velocity of an arrow.

"Hurry, Pinocchio!" cried the Goat, bleating loudly. And Pinocchio swam desperately with his arms, with his chest, with his legs, and with his feet.

"Hurry, Pinocchio, for the monster approaches you!" And Pinocchio, gathering his force, redoubled his strokes.

"Take care! take care! He is gaining! Hurry! Oh, hurry, or you are lost!" Pinocchio swam faster than ever, and away they both raced, going as fast as bullet balls. As they approached the rock the Goat held out its two front paws to aid Pinocchio to land. But —

It was too late! The monster had been too quick. Drawing in a quantity of water, he drank Pinocchio just as if he were sucking an egg. He swallowed him with such violence that the marionette arrived in the stomach of the Dogfish with such force that he was stunned for a quarter of an hour.

When he regained consciousness after being swallowed he did not know where he was. All around him was darkness so intense that he thought he had put his head into the top of an ink bottle. He listened but he heard nothing. From time to time he felt a great gust of wind striking his face. At first he did not know whence the wind came, but afterward he thought it was from the lungs of the monster; for you must know, my little readers, that the Dogfish was a great sufferer from asthma, and when he breathed it sounded like the north wind.

At first Pinocchio tried to be brave; but when he had tried and then tried again to find an exit and found himself still inclosed in the body of the monster, he began to cry and to scream: "Help! help! Oh, dear me! Is there no one who can save me?"

"Who wishes to be saved?" asked a voice that sounded in the darkness like a guitar out of tune.

"Who is it that speaks like that?" asked Pinocchio, feeling himself nearly frozen with fear.

"It is I. I am a poor Tunny fish, who was swallowed at the same time you were. What kind of fish are you?"

"I have nothing to do with fishes. I am a marionette."

"Then, if you are not a fish, why were you swallowed by the monster?"

"It is all your fault. If you had not been there, I surely should have escaped. And now what can we do in this dark place?"

"We must resign ourselves to our fate, and wait until we are digested."

"But I do not wish to be digested," said Pinocchio, beginning to cry.

"Neither do I wish to be digested," added the Tunny; "but I am philosopher enough to console myself by thinking that it is more dignified to die under water than to be soaking in vinegar and oil."

"Nonsense!" cried Pinocchio.

"It is my opinion," replied the Tunny; "and the opinion of fishes should be respected."

"As for me," said Pinocchio, "I wish to go away from here; I want to escape."

"Escape if you can."

"Is the Dogfish very large?" asked the marionette.

"Why, his body is a mile long without counting his tail."

In the meantime Pinocchio thought he saw in the distance a little glimmer of light.

"What can that be?" he asked.

"Some poor unfortunate that is probably being digested."

"Well, I am going to see. It may be some old fish that can tell me the way to walk around here."

"I wish you good luck, my poor marionette."

"Good-by, Tunny."

"Good-by, marionette, and good fortune go with you."

"When shall we meet again?"

"Who knows? It is better not to think of that."

CHAPTER XXXV

As soon as Pinocchio had said good-by to his friend the Tunny, he moved around, groping in the darkness. Walking inside the Dog-fish, he advanced toward the little light that shone so far away.

As he groped along he felt his feet wading in a puddle of greasy, slippery water. The water had such a pungent odor of fried fish that he thought it must be Lent.

The more he walked, the clearer and more distinct became the light, until finally he arrived at the end of the passage. What did he find? I will let you guess a thousand times. He found a little table all nicely set, and lighted by a candle stuck into a green bottle. Seated behind the table he saw an old man with snow-white beard and hair, who was slowly eating some little live fish.

At the sight of the poor old man Pinocchio became so overjoyed that he nearly lost his senses. He wished to laugh; he wished to cry. He did not

know what to do.   He finally murmured some joy-
ous sounds, for words stuck in his throat.   Giving
a cry of pleasure, he rushed to the old man, threw
his arms around his neck, and cried : " Oh, my dear
father !   At last I have found you !   Now I will
never leave you again, never, never, never ! "

"Do my eyes tell me truly ? " asked the old
man, rubbing them.   "Do I really see my dear
Pinocchio ? "

"Yes, yes ; it is I, truly, Pinocchio !   And you
have already forgiven me, have you not ?   Oh, my
papa !   How good you are !   And to think that I —
Oh, but if you only knew how many things have
happened to me, — how many troubles and trials !
Just imagine, the day you sold your coat for my
A B C card I ran away from school and met some
marionettes, and the manager wished to put me on
the fire so that I could cook some mutton that he
wanted to eat.   He gave me some pieces of gold
for you; but when I went toward home I met a
Fox and a Cat, who led me to an inn called the
Red Lobster, where they ate like wolves.   I left
the inn at night and met assassins who began to
run after me and finally caught me and hanged
me to a large oak.   Then a beautiful Fairy with
Blue Hair sent a carriage to take me to her house,
where there were doctors who said if I was not dead

it was a sign that I was alive. Then I told a lie and my nose commenced to grow so that I could not pass through the door of the room. After that I met the Fox and the Cat, who advised me to put the money in the ground and watch it grow. I lost it all, for I believed their story. When I told the judge of the town he put me in prison for being so foolish. After I was set free I walked along a road and, feeling hungry, I looked for a bunch of grapes; but I was caught in a trap and a farmer took me to his house and made me play dog. After I had caught the thieves that robbed his hencoop, he set me free; and I met a Serpent with a smoking tail, and it laughed so hard that it died. Then I hurried to the house of the beautiful Fairy, but she was gone. Oh, how unhappy I was! Then a Dove, seeing me cry, said to me, ' I have seen your papa making a ship to go and look for you '; and I said, ' Oh! if I had wings I would fly to him! ' And the Dove said, ' Get on my back '; and away we flew all night. The next day, when we arrived at the shore, the fishermen, looking toward the sea, said to me, ' There in that boat is a poor old man who will sink '; for the water was so rough. And I ran to a rock and recognized you, because my heart told me that you were there; and I made a sign for you to come back to the shore — "

"I recognized you also," said Geppetto, "and I would willingly have come back; but how could I?—the sea was so rough and my boat was so frail. Then a horrible Dogfish that was near me put out its tongue and swallowed me like a pill."

"And how long have you been shut up here?" asked Pinocchio.

"Two years, Pinocchio, that seemed like two centuries."

"And how have you lived? And where did you find the candle and the matches to light it?"

"I will tell you all. Fortunately, when the Dogfish swallowed me he swallowed also the provisions I had on board the ship—"

"What? He swallowed all in a mouthful?" asked Pinocchio, surprised.

"All in a mouthful. But he did not like the mast of the boat; for that stuck in his teeth like a toothpick and he spat that out. As the boat was loaded with preserved meat, figs, biscuits, wine, raisins, coffee, sugar, candles, and matches, I was well supplied. To-day, however, I am burning my last candle—"

"And after that?"

"Why, my dear boy, we shall both be left in the dark."

"Then, Papa," said Pinocchio, "there is no time to lose. We must hurry and escape."

" How ? "

" Why, we must escape from the mouth of the Dogfish and throw ourselves into the sea."

" But I do not know how to swim."

" That does not matter. You can get on my back and I will take you to the shore."

" You are dreaming, my boy," said Geppetto, shaking his head.

" Try it and see. Anyway, we shall have the consolation of dying together."

And without saying any more Pinocchio took the candle and started to walk toward the mouth of the Dogfish. " Come along, and do not be afraid, Papa," said Pinocchio.

And thus they walked along for a little while, traversing the whole length of the Dogfish's stomach. When they arrived at the end they stopped so as to look carefully before trying to escape.

Now, my little readers, you must know that the Dogfish, being very old and suffering from asthma and palpitation of the heart, was obliged to sleep with his mouth open. Pinocchio, therefore, looking up through the throat, saw the starry heavens and the light of the moon.

" This is truly the time to escape," whispered Pinocchio ; "the Dogfish sleeps and the sea is very

smooth.   Come, then, Papa.   Follow me and we
shall soon be outside."

No sooner said than done.   They mounted the
throat of the huge sea monster and, arriving in
the immense mouth, began to walk on the tips of
their toes along the tongue.   Suddenly the Dogfish sneezed.   The candle was blown out, and both
Geppetto and Pinocchio were given a violent shake
and found themselves back once more in the Dogfish's stomach.

"Now we are truly lost," said Geppetto.

"Give me your hand, and be careful not to slip."

"Where are you leading me?"

"Come along and do not be afraid."

Thus saying, Pinocchio took his papa's hand and
again they mounted the throat of the monster,
always going on tiptoe.   Then passing along the
tongue and the three rows of teeth, they found
themselves out in the air.

"Get on my back," said Pinocchio, "and hold on
tight."·

Scarcely had Geppetto placed his arms around
Pinocchio's neck when the brave marionette began
to swim.   The sea was as smooth as oil, the
moon was resplendent, and the Dogfish continued
to sleep so soundly that not even a cannon shot
would have awakened him.

CHAPTER XXXVI

While Pinocchio swam fast so as to reach the beach quickly, he perceived that his papa, who sat on his back, trembled just as if he had a high fever. Did he tremble from cold or fear? Who knows? Perhaps a little of both. But Pinocchio, believing that he trembled from fear, said to him in a comforting tone: "Courage, Papa! In a little while we shall arrive on the shore safe and sound."

"But where is the shore?" asked the old man, becoming more and more uneasy and straining his eyes to see it, just as tailors do when they thread a needle. "Here we are, swimming all night; and I see only sky and sea."

"But I see the shore," said the marionette. "Through your skill in making me, I can see in the night as well as a cat."

Poor Pinocchio pretended to be in good humor; but he was really beginning to lose heart. His strength was giving out and his breath growing shorter. In fact, he could not swim much longer and the shore could not be seen.

He swam until he had no more breath. Then he turned his head toward Geppetto and said in broken tones, " Help me, Papa, or I shall die."

The father and the boy were nearly drowned when they heard a voice, like a guitar out of tune, saying, " Who is going to die ? "

" My papa and I."

" I recognize that voice. You are Pinocchio."

" Exactly ; and who are you ? "

" I am Tunny, your companion in the Dogfish's stomach."

" How did you escape ? "

" I followed your example. You taught me the way ; and after I saw you go, I went also."

" Oh, my friend, you have come just in time! I pray you, for the love you bear your little tunny fishes, to help us, or we are lost."

" With all my heart! Get on my back and in a few minutes we shall reach land."

As you may easily imagine, Geppetto and Pinocchio quickly accepted the invitation.

" Are we too heavy ? " asked Pinocchio.

" Heavy ? Why, you are like two shadows. It seems to me that I have two small shells on my back."

When they arrived at the shore Pinocchio was the first to jump down, and he helped his papa. Then he turned to the Tunny and, with a voice that trembled with emotion, said : " My friend, you have saved my papa and me. I do not know how to thank you. Permit me to kiss you as a sign of eternal friendship."

The Tunny put his nose out of the water, and Pinocchio, kneeling on the ground, gave the fish an affectionate kiss. At this sign of tenderness the poor Tunny, who was not accustomed to such kindness, felt himself so moved that he began to cry like a baby, and quickly sank into the water to hide his tears.

In the meantime the sun arose. Then Pinocchio, offering his arm to his papa, who was very weak, said : " Lean on my arm, dear Papa, and let us go. We will walk just as slowly as ants, and when we are tired we will rest ourselves."

"And where shall we go ? " asked Geppetto.

" In search of a house where we can get a bit to eat and some straw to lie upon."

But they had not gone a hundred steps when they saw two ugly faces asking for money. They were the faces of the Fox and the Cat ; but one would not have recognized them. Just think ! the Cat who feigned to be blind had really become

so, and the Fox's hair was all shaggy and he had
lost his tail.

"Oh, Pinocchio," cried the Fox, "give a little
charity to two old people."

"Two old people," repeated the Cat.

"Good-by, masqueraders," replied Pinocchio;
"you deceived me once and now you are paying
for it."

"Believe us, Pinocchio, we are to-day truly poor
and starving."

"Truly," repeated the Cat.

"If you are poor, you deserve it. Remember the
proverb that says, 'Stolen money will never bear
fruit.' Good-by, deceivers!"

"Have compassion on us."

"On us," said the Cat.

"Good-by. Remember the proverb that says,
'Stolen wheat always makes poor bread.'"

"Do not abandon us."

"No, no!" said the Cat.

"Good-by. Remember the proverb, 'Whoever steals the cloak of his neighbor usually dies without a shirt.'"

Geppetto and Pinocchio continued their walk until they saw a small farmhouse with a straw roof.

"That house is inhabited by some one," said Pinocchio. "Let us go and knock at the door."

"Who is there?" said a voice inside, when they had reached the house.

"We are a poor papa and his son, without bread or a home," replied the marionette.

"Turn the key and the door will open," said the same voice.

Pinocchio turned the key and the door opened. As soon as they entered the house they looked around, but saw no one. "Where is the master of this house?" asked Pinocchio, greatly surprised.

"Here I am, up here."

Papa and son turned quickly and saw on a rafter the Talking Cricket.

"Oh, my dear Cricket!" said Pinocchio, saluting him politely.

"Now you call me your dear Cricket, do you not? Do you remember the time when you struck me with a hammer?"

"Yes, you were right, Cricket. Take a hammer and hit me, but spare my poor papa."

"I will have pity on you both ; but I wished to remind you of your ugly manners."

"Yes, Cricket, you were right to tell me what you did. You were right, and I will bear in mind the lessons you have taught me. But tell me, how did you build such a nice large house ? "

"This little house was given me yesterday by a beautiful Goat that had blue wool."

"And where has the Goat gone ? " asked Pinocchio, with lively curiosity.

"I do not know."

"And when will it return ? "

"Never. Yesterday it went away bleating. I thought I heard it say, ' Poor Pinocchio ! I shall never see him again. The Dogfish has swallowed him.' "

"It said that ? Then it was she. It was the beautiful Fairy," said Pinocchio, and he began to cry.

When he had cried a long time he dried his eyes and prepared a nice bed of straw for his papa. Then he said to the Talking Cricket, " Tell me, Cricket, where I can find a glass of milk for my poor papa."

"Three fields from here you will see a farmer who has cows. Go to him and you will find the milk you seek."

Pinocchio ran toward the farmer and said to him, "Will you please give me some milk?"

"How much do you want?"

"I want a glassful."

"A glass of milk costs one cent. Where is the money?"

"I have nothing," cried Pinocchio, mortified.

"If you have no money, I have no milk."

"I am so sorry!" said Pinocchio.

"Wait a minute," said the farmer; "I think we can arrange it. Do you know how to draw water from a well?"

"I can try."

"Well, draw me one hundred bucketfuls and I will give you a glass of milk."

"All right!"

Pinocchio worked so hard that when he had finished he was wet with perspiration from head to foot. He had never felt so tired in all his life.

"I have a little donkey that draws water for me; but to-day he is sick, poor thing!"

"May I see him?" asked Pinocchio.

"Certainly."

As soon as Pinocchio saw the donkey he recognized him. "I think I know that donkey," said he. Speaking to it in the donkey language, he asked, "Who are you?" At the question the donkey opened his eyes and replied in the same language, "I am Lamp Wick;" then he closed his eyes again.

"Oh, my poor Lamp Wick," said Pinocchio in an undertone; and then he took a little hay and gave it to him.

"Why do you take so much interest in a donkey that is not worth a cent?" asked the farmer.

"I will tell you. He was a friend of mine."

"Your friend?"

"Yes; a school companion."

"How is that?" asked the farmer, bursting into laughter. "You had donkeys for school companions?"

The marionette felt so mortified at these words that he took the glass of milk and returned to his papa.

From that day, for five months afterward, Pinocchio continued to get up in the morning at daybreak to draw water for the farmer; and he gained only a little milk for his trouble. He was not contented with simply doing that; he learned to make straw mats and sold them to buy food for his daily wants. Among other things, he made a little cart so that he could take his papa out and give him a little fresh air.

In the evenings he practiced reading and writing. In fact, he behaved so nicely that his papa was overjoyed. One morning he said to Geppetto: "I am going to market to buy a jacket, a cap, and a pair of shoes. When I come back I shall be dressed like a real gentleman."

Outside the house he began to run, because he was so happy. Suddenly he heard himself called by name, and, turning, he saw a beautiful Snail.

"Do you not know me?" asked the Snail.

"It seems to me— It seems to me—"

"Don't you remember the Snail that lived with the beautiful Fairy with the Blue Hair?"

"I remember all," cried Pinocchio. "Tell me quickly, where is the beautiful Fairy now?"

At these words the Snail replied with his usual siowness, "The beautiful Fairy lies ill in a hospital."

"In a hospital?"

"Yes. Wounded by so many misfortunes, she is very sick and so poor that she eats only a mouthful of bread each day."

"Truly? Oh, what a blow you have given me! Oh, my poor Fairy, my poor Fairy! If I had a million, I would give it all to you, but I have only forty cents, which I was going to use to buy some clothes. Take my money, Snail, and carry it quickly to the good Fairy."

"And what about your clothes?"

"What does that matter? I would sell these rags in order to help her. Go, Snail, and in two days come back, and I will have some more money for her."

The Snail began to get excited and ran as if a bird were after him.

When Pinocchio returned home his papa asked him, "Where are your new clothes?"

"I heard from the Snail that my good Fairy was ill in the hospital and so poor that she had no food, so I sent her the forty cents."

That night, instead of going to bed, Pinocchio worked until midnight. Afterward he went to bed and slept. And while he slept he thought he saw the good Fairy, all beautiful and happy and smiling, who, after giving him a kiss, said: "Good Pinocchio! For your good heart I pardon all your misdeeds. Boys that help their parents lovingly in their troubles always deserve praise and affection." Just here Pinocchio's dream ended and he awoke with his eyes opened wide.

Now imagine, little readers, the great surprise of Pinocchio, upon waking, to find that he was no longer a wooden marionette, but that he had become a boy like all the others! He gave a glance around him and, instead of a bed of straw, he saw a room beautifully furnished. Jumping down from his bed, he found prepared for him a nice new suit, a new cap, and a pair of new shoes.

He had scarcely dressed himself when, like all boys who have a new suit, he put his hands into his pockets; and just imagine his surprise when he pulled out a small pocketbook of mother-of-pearl, on which were written these words: "The Fairy with the Blue Hair returns the forty cents to her dear Pinocchio and thanks him with all her heart." Opening the pocketbook, he found, instead of forty pennies, forty pieces of gold.

Afterward he went to look in the looking-glass and he did not know himself. He saw no longer the reflection of a wooden marionette, but the image of a bright and intelligent boy with chestnut hair and large bright eyes. Pinocchio was greatly surprised. In the midst of these marvels that happened one after another he did not know whether it was all real or whether it was a dream.

"Where is my papa?" he cried suddenly. Then, entering the next room, he found Geppetto well and as young as when he first began his profession of carving.

"What does it all mean, dear Papa?" asked Pinocchio.

"It means that you must try to deserve all this beautiful house," said Geppetto.

"I *will* try," said Pinocchio. "And why is it that you look so well and young?"

"Because when bad boys become good, they cause everything to change for the better and make the whole family happy."

"And the old wooden Pinocchio — where is it hidden?"

"There it is," replied Geppetto, pointing to a wooden marionette leaning on a chair with its head limp, its arms hanging down, and its legs crossed, so that it was a wonder that it could stand at all.

Pinocchio turned to look at his old self; and after he had regarded it a little while, he said with great satisfaction: "How naughty I was when I was a marionette! and how happy I am now that I have become a real live boy!"

a 13487
1300
─────
50

ROBINSON CRUSOE
NIGHTS
SWISS FAMILY ROBINSON
TALES FROM SHAKESPEAR